Lost American Fiction

In 1972 the Southern Illinois University Press republished Edith Summers Kelley's *Weeds*. Its reception encouraged the Press to mount a series that would republish obscure or unavailable works of fiction that merit a new audience. Since 1972 eighteen volumes of Lost American Fiction have appeared—in hardbound from the Southern Illinois University Press and in paperback from Popular Library, the cooperating publisher.

The editor is frequently asked about the basis for selection. There can be no clear guidelines, for the decisions are largely subjective. The only rule is that to be considered for publication a book must have been originally published at least twenty-five years ago. Our chief consideration, of course, has been literary merit. Another quality we are looking for might be called "life": does the work live?—does it have a voice of its own?—does it present human nature convincingly? A third test for including a work in the series is its historical value: does it illuminate the literary or social history of its time? The volumes chosen so far do not represent one editor's judgment: some were recommended by colleagues, our cooperating publisher, and by strangers who responded to the concept of the series.

At this point the editor and publisher feel that the Lost American Fiction series has largely achieved what it set out to do. Eighteen novels have been given another chance, and some have found new audiences. The paperback reprint arrangement with Popular Library is making the books available to a wide readership. To be sure, some will vanish again. We cannot claim that all of the titles are lost masterpieces, but we believe that some of them are. There has been considerable disagreement from readers about individual titles. We never expected uniformity of response. That readers would find the Lost American Fiction books worth reading and would be prompted to make their own appraisals is all we wanted.

M. J. B.

LOST AMERICAN FICTION
Edited by Matthew J. Bruccoli

Inn of That Journey

by
Emerson Price

Afterword by the Author

3191

SOUTHERN ILLINOIS UNIVERSITY PRESS
Carbondale and Edwardsville

Feffer & Simons, Inc.
London and Amsterdam

Library of Congress Cataloging in Publication Data

Price, Emerson.
  Inn of that journey.

  (Lost American fiction)
  Reprint of the ed. published by Caxton Printers, Caldwell, Idaho.
  I. Title.
PZ3.P9306In9 [PS3531.R5147]   813'.5'2
ISBN 0-8093-0812-6   77-23199

The author would like the new edition of this work to commemorate the memory of his beloved daughter, Lynne Price, who believed the novel has both literary and social value. And she believed in her father as, indeed, he deeply believed in her.

Peace is the heir of dead desire
Whether abundance killed the cormorant
In a happy hour, or sleep or death
Drowned him in dreamy waters,
Peace is the ashes of that fire,
The heir of that king, the inn of that journey.

—Robinson Jeffers,
"Suicide's Stone"

*The earth beneath his body...
was as soft as a feather pillow.
He scooped a layer of dusty
topsoil away and thrust his hot,
sweaty cheek into the cool subsoil.... (Charlie Heston...
had said that some men feel a
deep kinship for the soil; that
is part of their being)....Now,
Mark sifted dust through his
fingers. It was like dry sand
and he was conscious of the
musty, earthy smell of the moist
soil beneath....No odor on
earth could please his senses so
much....*

1

IT WAS still early morning. An insistent April breeze set a loose windowpane to snapping; and the chirping of sparrows in the tall, gaunt trees outside pierced the agonizing silence. The drawn green window shade moved without noise, and only a faint, early-morning light reached softly for the floor beneath. The room seemed a vacuum into which a multitude of noises was attempting to creep.

The woman lay motionless, her face drawn with fatigue. It was a white face with bright, frightened eyes which bored into the gloom about it. Strangely mature, it nevertheless bore a curious resemblance to that of a child. Her soft brow was knitted, but the fine lines running through the forehead were not those of annoyance so much as fear. And the look of fear had always been there. Dark patches beneath the eyes gave them a burning, haunted look.

Presently she turned her head and looked at the wrinkled creature who had so lately torn her loins in an agony of pain. He had made queer noises when she heaved him into the world. Now the breath of life had fastened itself to him, and he slept so softly that she could not hear him. Only the snapping windowpane and chirping birds bellowed against the dark wall of silence. The woman went to weeping softly. Then she set her small jaws, sending the loose skin about her face into a tiny ludicrous pucker. The effort seemed pitiable and weak.

Now she was visited by a momentary vision in which a clear understanding of the finality of death came to her. Raising her hand, she curled her fingers and looked at them with wonder in her eyes.

Her brain leaped to escape something. It battered her skull. She was momentarily paralyzed with fear and with the realization that there is no escape. Then the spell was broken by the memory of a laugh and the words of the baby's father. She flushed with anger and embarrassment. It was over, and he looked, did the father, and he laughed.

"He's got balls like a young bull," said he. And then he laughed again until her sobs rolled out in choked noises. He had no sense of discretion and never would have, she thought. Now hoofbeats battered the wall of early morning and she remembered that Sawyer Haines must be going to the depot to meet the five-twenty. And a train whistled far down the road, and rolling iron wheels sent a rumbling into the vacuum. A man whistled just outside the door. She closed her eyes.

Presently the door opened noiselessly and a man thrust his head inside. He grinned, plucked thoughtlessly at a mole on his nose, and closed the door again. He looked out of a window and drew on a pair of work gloves. His hands were small. When he looked from the window he could see that there were buds on the tall maple trees in the front yard.

Look down and look back. And what dark thing did that woman give you, boy? What did you keep from the seed of the dead? What led you into strange paths and what were you searching for—and why? O sleeping fellow, you did not know that you would live a thousand lives and puzzle about them all. There were to be pictures and patterns in your curious mind, and a strange insanity was to clutch you all your days.

Clop! Clop! Clop! Get along, old horse, and pull that buggy with you. For your days, too, are numbered. The sleeping fellow will see you change, and the world will change and the permanent things that greet a white-haired boy are in the attics of a thousand cities.

And why did they kill Wickie? He rocked into limp, dead flesh, and a blue flame fried the blood in his veins. What if he did like to rip dead fish with his bare hands and pant like a dog when the blood came out? He was crazy. You knew that. Nutsie lay in bed for fifteen years with legs wasted and paralyzed. And Soapy, too. He died alone with a great hunk of tobacco stuffed in his cheek. He spat a stream of amber juice as the pain lessened and a film reached over his eyes. He remembered singular things in an old world. Voices that he had not heard for years bellowed in his ears, and a great darkness swallowed him.

Blood is strewn on the streets of a thousand cities, boy. And you were there. Only the sweetness of a white-haired boy who laughed at the sky remains. And there were tall trees, too.

The men who sat on bread boxes and talked of the possibilities of William Howard Taft are gone. Their secrets are buried with them. Or they are hobbling old men who look with faded eyes into the mists of long ago. And they see nothing. Even you are not there. But there is a memory of an old man sitting on a porch and playing a guitar. And music goes softly into a dark, dark valley before him. And presently he spits off the porch and walks into his kitchen. It is lighted by the feeble flame of an old oil lamp.

And old Hump Bing with his cabin far back in the orchard. Why did he rape that pretty young woman? Old Hump with his crooked back and only half a foot on his right leg and his evil face and foul breath. With a mind as crooked as his body he died in the penitentiary.

Now you piece together tiny bits of broken memory. It was just the rustling of leaves outside your window long ago in summer. You remember that. And the soft dark night.

There was love and strangeness and shame. Now there are old women with creviced cheeks and painful rheumy bodies and hordes of grown children with children of their own. The soft flesh is soggy and jaundiced. Wisps of thin white hair. Bald-headed men near middle-life with the pudgy fatness of success hanging to them.

Now walk in the rain, little boy, and listen sadly to the melancholy patter of raindrops as they snap against the dry dead leaves of autumn. There are barren hillsides lying in brown death. Ah, boy —you are a strange one to feel that way. There are things being said to you, boy, and you do not hear.

Race into the late summer darkness. Run over hillsides. Flee from something.

In the cornfield you scooped away the dry dust and put your hot cheek against the damp soil beneath. The musty odor of clean earth. You are the soil, and you love the soil.

Did you have comrades? Aye, a few. You were a fool, for suffering never changed you. It was in the strange seed of those who spend a million years of life. It was transmitted to you—it is of you and of them.

Sleep on, boy, and your frightened mother, too. Your soft baby breath is sweet. It is all ahead. And there will be whisky, and a thousand storms will batter the walls of time. You will be there to curse the madness. It will come. Sleep on.

Mark Cullen could never remember all of it. But broken bits of the past did come back to him. And then he wondered at the waste of time to let so much of life slip into nothingness. For there were years that dropped that dark blanket. As maturity approached the events of his life dotted memory like a long row of trees, but early childhood was a desolate field of scattered images reaching back into eternity.

His father, he knew, called his mother Judy, and later he learned that her name was Judith. But when Mark spoke to her he called her Mama. His father's name was Michael, and his mother called him by that name. To the boy he was Papa. As he grew older he shortened the names of his parents to Mom and Pop.

His father's temper, quick and violent, spent itself in short bursts of fury. His laughter burst from him in choking, uneven spasms. It startled those who heard it. Fighting its way through his throat, it came forth in unearthly noises, while the great force of it rocked his belly like an earthquake. But Michael did not often laugh. The anger of Judy was sharp, but at the same time puny and ineffectual. It usually ended in a fit of weeping which sometimes took on the aspects of melodrama.

There were things Mark knew, but never could trace the origin of the knowledge to any first event.

They were simple things. Each morning his father fed and milked two cows in the rickety old barn back of the house. He fed the horse and the chickens. There were rows of crocks filled with cream in the cellar, and twice each week his mother churned this into rich, yellow butter.

Each day his father hitched the horse to a buggy and drove away from home, and each evening he returned. On cold winter days he wore great, fur gloves and covered himself in the open vehicle with a huge bearskin robe.

The robe he tossed on the floor before an open grate fire in the front room. It was here that Mark lay down to sleep when the evening meal was done.

His father grumbled a good deal, and his mother constantly explained in a defensive manner. But there were times when Michael's voice seemed confiding while that of Judy was sympathetic.

Grandpa and Grandma Keenan lived across the road, and Mark sometimes stayed with them while his parents were away. The old man had white whiskers and a fringe of white hair about a shiny, bald head. He had a bellowing voice and never smiled. But sometimes he burst into roaring laughter that rolled and boomed through the house like thunder. The laughter always ended suddenly, leaving a heavy silence behind it.

Grandma was mild and quiet and never became angry. Sometimes the old man hitched his horse to an open buggy and drove away. When he came home he always had two huge bottles stuffed in his coat pocket. His roaring return sent Mark's grandmother to weeping.

But these things were not clear and sharp, and they had nothing to do with memory. They were not things he remembered, but things he knew. They seemed a permanent part of life like the people in his small world.

His earliest recollection seemed a momentary opening in a dark blanket. Through the rent he caught a fleeting glimpse of the world before darkness closed over him again. His age at the time was always a matter of doubt, though he probably was not yet three.

It was winter, and he stood before a window. A man walked across an open field. Now and then he stopped and stomped his feet. He swung his arms and thumped his gloved hands together, and Mark knew that it was cold in the grey out of doors. At the far end of the field there were naked trees whose branches swayed clumsily in the wind. Beyond the trees were houses.

Suddenly a wall of yellow flame rolled from the top of one of the houses, and a woman ran from the door, waving her arms wildly. She wore an apron. The man walking across the field now burst into a run toward the flaming building.

"Mama," said Mark. "The house is burning."

He said this simply and without excitement. His mother ran to him and looked out the window.

"Why, it's Carr's house!" she said with startled suddenness. "Now you stay right here by the window. I'll only be gone a minute."

She threw a cape about her shoulders and ran from the door. A great silence swept over Mark. He did not want to be left alone, and the flaming house seemed far away. He had wanted her to watch with him and to explain why the fire rolled from the top of the building.

Mark remembered that she returned, but the remainder of the picture became indistinct. Shadows drooped over it, and darkness followed. He remembered nothing until the following spring.

Mark slept in a little bed with side rails. Often his mother rocked him to sleep. And when she did this she sang to him softly.

The look of fright on his mother's features he could not comprehend. Sometimes she successfully masked that look with tiny frowns. But more often the old haunted look was there. And it was not a thing she herself could explain. It was an unreasonable portent of danger that always lay in the offing.

"What's the matter, Mama?" Mark sometimes asked her.

And she, caught unawares, promptly sealed the vaults of thought with a small frown.

"Oh, nothing, son," she explained. "I'm just a little worried. What made you think there was anything the matter?"

"I don't know. I just thought there was."

Mark thought his mother very pretty, and he wondered what cause she had for fright. He remembered seeing a red squirrel whose leg was caught in a steel trap. It had that same terrified look as it lay, huddled and still, awaiting the knife of the trapper.

> "Way down by the rock in the meadow,
> The brook ripples by with a song. . . . "

When his mother sang this Mark thought of the little stream back of the house and of the deep ravine where the tops of tall trees barely reached the crest of the steep slope. He liked it there. He liked the silence which clung to the place.

He sat in his high chair at supper. Michael and Judy carried on a desultory conversation. On Mark's plate were meat and potatoes. The meat had been cut into bites. He selected the largest hunk, crammed it into his mouth, chewed a moment, and then swallowed. The meat did not go down. He swallowed again and then tried to breathe. He sat for a moment, his eyes bulging. He tried again and again.

His face bulged like an inflated balloon, and a terrible agony closed over his tiny body. The table swam before his eyes, and the voices of his parents drifted—drifted until they seemed far away. He kicked and struggled.

His father sat tensely and without motion, but his mother seized him and beat his back soundly. The boy scarcely felt the blows. A moment—a moment—then the lump of cooked beef, stringy and moist, flew from his mouth. . . . A gust of clean air burst into his tortured lungs as the lad lay limp and helpless in his mother's arms.

"God, I thought he was gone!" said Michael.

And for the first time the boy knew that the dark eternity of the past would someday reclaim him. It had reached out a black hand and withdrawn it empty.

Mark Cullen grew in time to a thoughtful youngster, and while Michael provided each day an abundance of food, the lad took on all the appearances of an undernourished child. He wandered about the fields with a curious loneliness hanging about him. In his puzzled mind were strange images, and on his tongue were questions which could not be answered.

Incidents which punctured the vacuum of memory to implant themselves on the walls of his mind became more frequent. Early in life he asked himself and others, "Why am I here?" Throughout most of the years of his early childhood, he thought grown people held the answer to the riddle of life.

When he passed by the village grocery with his father his eyes were wide with amazement at the men who sat on bread boxes before it, talking. He wanted to sit with them and hear their great talk. He did not believe that they were riffraff as Michael so often insisted.

At the beginning of his fourth summer the incidents of his life became marked and definite. Many things were not of sufficient interest to penetrate the vaults of his mind and remain there. But those things which did impress him remained with him throughout his life.

It was during this period that he first saw and remembered a plowed field. Michael hired Jim McLain to prepare the field for corn. And Mark watched the dark, rich soil curl into long furrows behind the plowshare. Strong horses pulled the plow, and the furrows rolled like serpents. The clean smell of upturned earth assailed his nostrils in a pleasing wave.

At night in his little bed he listened to the breath of summer. From the darkness of the night came the quiet rustling of leaves on the trees in the yard. Voices were sometimes carried to him gently through the darkness. Soft and low, they seemed at the same time throbbing with life.

"Summer is alive," he thought.

But the sunless days of autumn brought to him a feeling of sadness which he could never translate into common language.

One day in the grey and melancholy autumn he walked back to the ravine. The wind ripped leaves from the trees and sent them flying into brown wastes of dead grass. And rain struck his face like hard pebbles. He felt homeless and alone. Careless of wind and rain alike, he walked through the soggy bottoms along the brook until he reached the wide and winding river two miles away.

There he stood alone, a tiny, huddled, human creature groping into the darkness with his child mind. He watched the muddy water before him sweeping angrily onward, carrying with it the debris of a thousand fields to the north. The wet, bare branches of the trees along the river swayed in the wind. Their skeleton limbs rattled.

Fearful that the black night would fall before he reached home, he left the place. The fear in him mounted, and he ran through the rain. Cold water ran down his back, and his clothing was drenched. Michael and Judy had been searching for him. They were frightened.

"You little fool," shouted Michael. "Where have you been?"

The boy's wasted figure trembled. His bedraggled clothing clung to his tiny frame like those of a scarecrow. He could find no words for his lonely adventure, and he shook with sobs.

"I—I—took a walk," he blubbered.

"The devil of a day for a walk!" bellowed Michael. "Now the truth! Where were you?"

Judy interrupted. She undressed him, bathed the chill from his trembling body, and wrapped him in warm blankets.

"Where were you, son? Where did you go?" she asked.

"I just wanted to see the river, and I walked down there," he said.

"I understand, son," she whispered. "But you mustn't do it any more. You worried Mama."

Mark Cullen was still in bed when the first icy blasts of winter roared out of the northwest. He recovered from pneumonia, and the following autumn he started to school.

Grandma Keenan died suddenly. And Mark learned then that death is brutal and without compromise. He learned that it is without dignity and that its processes are horrible to witness. He learned these things quite accidentally.

In the confusion he slipped unnoticed into the room with the corpse. A group of women were preparing the body for services and burial. They were winding a sheet about his grandmother's naked legs. They all talked at once so that there was a confusion of words. Meantime Grandma Keenan's legs were bobbing about in the air like those of a fowl being stuffed for the roast. In a quick and horrified glance he saw that her mouth was open and that her unseeing eyes were open. They looked like blue lumps of jelly. Shaking with terror, he ran from the room.

He remembered the incident poignantly for weeks. He remembered it with the thought that Grandma wouldn't want anyone to see her like that.

Twenty-five years later he remembered her stiffened and bobbing legs when a coroner in northern Ohio sawed the top from the head of a murdered man and removed the brain.

"A few days ago the old bastard wouldn't have looked so unconcerned about it," said the coroner. And a woman attendant at the morgue laughed. And the coroner flopped the dead man's scalp over his face so that the hair dropped into the opened eyes and mouth.

Mark wanted the assurance and what appeared to be the wisdom of his elders. It was this impulse that nearly cost his life. And throughout all the years that followed, he never forgot that grim adventure.

On his way to school he heard a railroad engine shriek, and his ears caught plainly the rumbling of iron wheels. He remembered the words of cautious Judy, and his impulse was to wait. Before him a man raced across the track. Mark leaped forward and followed.

In a final moment he halted in utter confusion as the monster raced toward him. In wild panic he turned back, stopped again, and then leaped toward the oncoming engine and certain death.

The powerful arms of a farmer dragged Mark from the groaning rails. Leaping from a near-by wagon, the man swept him to safety as the rumbling wheels cleared the crossing. Huddled and trembling, Mark saw distinctly the features of the engineer. The look of terror in the man's face remained with him throughout his life.

In just a momentary glance Mark saw distinctly his blackened goggles, his open mouth and the sickly white face showing forth under patches of grease. He saw, too, that an edge of his jacket, hanging from the cab window, fluttered in the wild wind.

All this he saw and remembered for years. But

the face of his rescuer and his name he could not remember. That fellow who risked everything to save the life of a child was driven almost instantly from the walls of the boy's mind. And he never could explain this.

2

S O THE YEARS rolled up in that quiet, peaceful village, and Mark slowly grew into an older boy.

Michael Cullen, a supervisor in public township schools, worried once each year.

Michael worried over what members of the Board of Education might do when it came that time of year to rehire him. When that period was successfully past Michael settled back for another year of comfort and quiet. He read his paper at evening, plucked at the mole on his nose, and lived peacefully enough. He complained a great deal, but that was part of the man. He could not be otherwise. He was not always just with his wife and boy, but he meant to be. And he thought he was.

But the day came when the Board of Education did not rehire him, and Michael cast about for another job. He got that business over with as soon as possible so that he would not have to worry about it. Michael Cullen certainly did not like to worry.

This moving away from the old house where Mark Cullen was born was like a trip to Mars. It was like a trip to Mars without the possibility of ever coming back. The old house was the beginning of all things. Mark was twelve now, but already an eternity lay between him and his first dim recollections.

Far back in time he remembered the giant forms of maple trees that stood like sentinels in the front yard. A great catalpa stood there, too. Its trunk was divided near the ground, and two sets of branches rose in the air like ungainly arms reaching for the sky. With a feeling of contentment and well-being the boy had listened to the quiet, sweeping rustle of their leaves on dark, summer nights. A multitude of summer noises often lulled him to sleep. It was like music from some vast symphony; remote and far away.

Sometimes his memory did not regard time. It leaped from season to season rapidly. He remembered bitter-cold winter nights and the warmth of the old barn. There, lantern in hand, he followed his father and milked one of the cows while his father milked the other. The old structure rattled and creaked in bitter winds, but the cold fury could not penetrate. The boy would squat on a one-legged stool, listening abstractedly to the swish-swish of the hay that had been fed to the cows, and to the horse crunching corn.

Michael's expert hands brought forth great streams of milk, and they rattled in the bottom of the pail like the noisy roll of a snare drum. Mark's boy hands squeezed out little, thin, inaudible jets. It was a slow task for him, but he liked it. He thrust his head into the cow's side and gazed down at the slowly filling bucket. There was comfort in the old barn ... on cold winter nights.

Rainy days. Then Mark explored old forgotten things in the attic. The attic was unfinished and had a stationary ladder leading up to it. It had that warm, dry atmosphere one attaches to old things. He rummaged there and dreamed great dreams of people and things belonging to a time long before.

He looked at old tintype photographs of stern-visaged men, some in uniform; nearly all of them heavily bearded. Sometimes the naked, foolish face of an unbearded man showed forth, and he imagined the fellow must have been a strange creature in a world of bearded men.

The women were strange and grotesque with clumsily knotted hair, and with tiny hats tilted over their eyes. They wore huge, bulging bustles which distorted them oddly. About their wasplike waists they wore tiny doll jackets. Their eyes looked forth vaguely from a piece of tin.

Sometimes Mark would carry a picture to his mother and inquire whom it might represent.

"That is your great-uncle," she would say. "He is dead."

Or, "That is my oldest sister. She is dead."

And the boy learned that most of those strange people were already forgotten. This added a new glamor to the only things left of them.

Now the Cullen family was to move away from all this. Because he knew he must go, Mark took a new interest in the old house. He wandered through each room. He felt a little lonely, saying good-by to the only world he had ever known. He looked at the highly polished black walnut woodwork. It was quaintly carved. He traced the curious designs with longing eyes and wished that he might take it all along with him. He was certain that no other house in the world had such lovely woodwork.

It was autumn, and in other years the family would have made apple butter in the back yard. Mark would have stirred it all day in a copper kettle with a long-handled ladle. There would have been a slow wood fire kept burning all day. Michael would have been storing food in the huge, musty cellar under the house. And there would have been hogs to butcher—sweet hams cured in hickory smoke. But not now. The old house had been sold.

One of the cows had been sold; the other Michael was to take with them. Michael owned only one horse, which he used for both work and driving. He had been successful in landing another rural school district in a township twenty miles away. The Cullens were going to live in Scatterfield, Ohio.

Mark did not anticipate the change with much

enthusiasm. When he asked his mother her face showed traces of distress.

"It is a wretched place," she said.

But not so with Michael. He had educated himself, and though he had taken up schoolwork, his whole being was deeply rooted in the soil. He sometimes became sentimental about the hardships he had endured for the sake of his schooling. An education, he said, was worth every privation one might be obliged to endure to attain it.

"I was a poor boy," he would say, "and I got no encouragement at home. My father could neither read nor write, but he had a good mind. I worked twelve and fourteen hours a day during the hot summer in a stone quarry. I saved my money and went to school in the winter. I studied all night sometimes, and worked all the next day. I was poor, and I had no encouragement."

And then Judith, puckering her mouth so that ludicrous little wrinkles coursed through her cheeks, would answer, "And you aren't rich yet, either."

"There's no need of complaining," stormed Michael, clubbing the floor with pacing feet and swinging his arms in a gesture of eloquence. "I cannot choose my work. I must live where I can. It won't hurt you to live there. The town is better than anything I knew until I was well along in life."

"I'm not complaining," sighed Judith. "I merely said the place is wretched. It is."

But with all Michael's burst of eloquence in defense of education, and despite the glorification of his hectic youth, which was patterned somewhat after the more puerile biographies of Abraham Lincoln, he was essentially a peasant. His greatest joy in life came from his ability to make the soil produce in abundance. He cultivated corn and potatoes with a passionate pleasure. He hoed his gardens with sweat streaming from his face, but with the satisfaction that only a peasant can know. He knew the art of crop rotation long before it became a part of American university curriculum.

In later years in Scatterfield, and with the aid of manures and other fertilizers, fine gardens sprang from that barren, yellow soil. Michael labored diligently and with intelligence. For him life held no satisfaction unless with hand and brain he might produce living things from the soil. Even his spirit of frugality was analogous with that of the peasant. He produced food from the soil and stored it against the heavy needs of winter, but with money he was a child.

Mark slept but little that night. The house had an empty look with its bare floors and vacant, staring windows. Voices rolled lugubriously through the rooms and hallways to come back in dull, toneless echoes—urging the Cullens to be gone.

The furniture was piled about in handy places to be loaded next morning on three hay wagons which Michael had hired for the occasion. It rained during the night, and Mark listened to the melancholy patter of the drops outside his window. The leaves were falling from the trees in the yard, and a strong wind blew them against the windowpane. Raindrops snapped against those still clinging to the trees, beating them down, leaving tall, black skeletons to stand alone in the yard until next spring.

Toward morning the rain stopped, and Mark heard his mother downstairs. As he got up he heard the wagons backing up to the door. It would be several hours before daybreak, and the journey to Scatterfield and back would take the drivers all day. The weather still looked uncertain, and each driver carried a canvas cover for the furniture in case of rain.

When the furniture was all loaded Mark noticed with annoyance that the mattress to his own bed was placed on top of the heap. It was stained from frequent bed-wetting and, Mark thought, advertised that unpleasant fact too obviously. He was embarrassed, but said nothing.

Michael and Judy drove on in the buggy. They left Mark to ride on Jim McLain's wagon. The boy was to sit on the back end and lead the cow.

He was glad of this, for he liked Jim. Jim was a little man whose shoulders were stooped. His face was deeply creviced and weather-beaten.

His arms were long and flapped about madly when he walked, like the arms of a scarecrow in the wind. His hands were large and muscular. They were always covered with a fine, grey dust. They were the hands of a teamster. Jim was not yet twenty-five, but there was a great work hump on his back, and his wrinkled neck seemed to grow straight out of his chest.

He chewed plug tobacco, and his lips were always stained with the juice. He often grinned foolishly, exposing a partial set of uneven yellow teeth. Some of his front teeth were missing. He had the mind of a child and talked as gravely and earnestly to Mark as he did to anyone else. He asked the boy's opinion on various matters and listened attentively to his replies. He made Mark feel important, and he liked the fellow for it.

Jim's wagon was the last to leave. It rumbled out over the hard stone pike. The horses walked slowly. They were fine, big, muscular animals and pulled the heavily loaded wagon with ease. The large iron-tired wagon wheels rattled over the road, and the slow clickety-clack of the horses' ironshod hoofs disturbed the stillness of early morning. They passed the schoolhouse, which Mark could see dimly outlined in the dark. It would be many hours before the yard would be full of eager, shouting children. Now it seemed singularly deserted and useless.

Mark sat hunched on the back of the wagon, his legs dangling next to the lighted lantern. He held tightly to the rope which led the cow, and he could see her slow, awkward figure moving patiently on and on through the dark. Her huge udder swayed painfully from side to side with each ungainly step she took.

The wagon passed over the brook where Mark had fished so many times with a bent pin and black thread fastened to a short hickory pole. And now the boy passed out beyond the kindly influence of the old house and plodded slowly toward a new world. He lost something there which in all the world he never recovered.

The lad grew tired and tethered the cow to the back of the wagon. He squirmed and wriggled through the furniture and went up to sit beside Jim. Jim was just biting a hunk of tobacco out of a plug.

"Give me a chew, will you, Jim?" Mark asked.

"Sure," said Jim. "Sure thing."

He wiped his nose on the sleeve of his coat and handed the tobacco to Mark. The boy bit into it. It tasted sweet and bit into his tongue. He chewed it furiously and spat great jets of amber juice.

"By God!" said Mark. "That there is good tobacco."

"I al'ys chew it," said Jim gravely.

A few drops of rain brushed Mark's cheek, and Jim yelled "Whoa!" to the horses. The wagons ahead stopped, too, and the drivers got out and stretched canvas over the furniture. Jim stretched the canvas, saving enough to the front for a rain shelter. Mark's throat felt dry, and he spat often. He swallowed enough to moisten his throat.

It was growing light now, and Jim blew out the lantern. Mark and Jim both climbed back on the wagon, pulling the cover over their heads. Mark felt dizzy, and the road heaved up and down before his eyes. He wanted to get rid of his chew and could think of no graceful way to do it. His stomach churned, and he retched a little.

"I guess I better go back and look after that cow, Jim," he finally said.

"Good idy," Jim agreed.

Mark crawled painfully back through the jungle of chairs and tables and stoves. The muscles in his abdomen jerked spasmodically. He lay down on his belly, his head thrust beneath a chair and his mouth closely fitted to a wide crack in the floor of the wagon. He knew Jim could not hear him and retched violently. His face, even his hair, was drenched with cold sweat. He vomited. He gasped and choked as it burst through his nostrils, stopping his breath. He took a deep breath and vomited again.

He turned his face sideways and looked beneath the canvas. The cow still lumbered along behind, her head thrust close to the ground. Occasionally she tugged at the rope in an effort to free herself. Rain poured over her and ran to the ground in little rivulets. It beat a sharp tattoo on the canvas above the boy's head. The wagon shook and jolted.

Mark heard Jim call to the horses. He reflected that Jim knew how to handle horses. He talked to them a good bit, and never used a whip. The boy cushioned his head on his arm. Beyond that he was too weak to move. Finally his stomach quieted down a bit, and he dropped asleep.

When Mark awakened the wagon had stopped. He heard Jim McLain walking in the road. The canvas flapped, and rain fell steadily. The boy still felt weak, but his stomach seemed better. The sense of nausea was gone—except when he reflected on his recent introduction to tobacco. Jim called.

"This danged cow has balked, Mark," he said, "an' we'll have to git out an' drive 'er."

"All right, Jim. I'll skutch her legs an' make 'er git along."

Mark crawled out of his shelter and into the rain. It was daylight, but that kind of daylight that comes in bleak Ohio autumns. It did not seem that the rain could ever stop. Mark had no rain-

coat, and Jim loaned him one. It was so long that
Mark could not wear it, so he threw it over his
head. He took Jim's long blacksnake whip and
wrapped it vigorously around the cow's legs. She
moved on stubbornly. She was tired. She had
never walked so far in her life.

The wagon shook and rattled and jolted over
the hard stone pike. Occasionally it struck a chuck-
hole, and the pile of furniture atop careened ominously. The cow had to be lashed now with nearly
every step. Mark cursed her loudly. His vocabulary in profanity was extensive. He liked to swear,
but he was careful that Michael never overheard
him. It was easy to swear in Jim's presence, though.
Jim recognized no tangible difference between
children and men. Mark cursed before Jim with a
good deal of confidence and not a little pride.

Mark splashed on and on. His shoes were wet
through, and the bottoms of his overalls were
soaked. The wind and rain beat into his face. He
grew tired and felt weak from vomiting. Mile after
mile he trudged, and his curses grew less frequent.
His legs ached to the hips, and the manly occupa-
tion of driving a stubborn cow through the rain
lost much of its zest. Tears and rain streamed
down his face.

Finally Jim stopped the horses and got down
from the wagon. They were in a flat country,
dotted with neat farmhouses. Mark watched smoke

roll comfortably from their chimneys through the
cold and ceaseless rain. Jim walked back to Mark.
The lad was numb with cold.

"Are you gittin' tired walkin'?" he asked.

"Hell, no," Mark lied.

"Well, I'm gittin' powerful tired a-settin', and
I'll walk a spell if you'll drive the team."

Mark was too eager to conceal it.

"Sure!" said he.

He climbed up to the wagon seat and took up
the lines. It wasn't every day that a boy got a
chance to drive a fine team like this one. He felt
grateful to Jim for entrusting it to him. He
hunched his body like that of a true teamster and
clicked at the team.

"Get up there, damn you!" said he.

The horses swept into a powerful and rhythmical
walk. Their heads nodded up and down in unison,
and Mark watched the muscles in their great rumps
swell and roll. Jim always had fine horses. They
were well-groomed and well-trained. The driver
never had to whip them. They were alert. Sometimes Jim talked harshly to them and cracked the
whip, but he saw to it that even the tip end of the
lash never touched their glossy hides. At night
when he unharnessed them he spent a long time
rubbing them. He fed them well and bedded them
with fresh, clean straw. Mornings he spent an
hour currying and brushing them. They were al-

ways spick and span. They were beautiful animals.

Mark felt proud to be their temporary master. He watched the foaming sweat roll from beneath their saddle pieces and dissolve in the rain. The two wagons ahead rolled slowly on. It was like a caravan sweeping slowly into a vast and unknown country.

Mark now viewed the situation with a spirit of adventure and wondered what his new home would be like. He wondered about the school and the kids. The next day would be Saturday, and he wouldn't be obliged to go to school. He thought nervously of entering the school Monday. The first day of school is an ordeal for the new kid.

The wagons rolled for many miles through a flat, monotonous country where Mark could see a great distance. The monotony was relieved only by an occasional gaunt, naked tree or a haystack with canvas top. The caravan passed great fields of corn stubble with rows and rows of cornshocks. Uneven fields lay about, filled with dead vegetation. They had been gardens in the summer and had been harvested long since.

It was late afternoon when the wagons turned into a muddy side road to the left. Mark drove Jim's team into the yellow, oozy mud. The horses labored now, for the mud was thick and sticky. The wide wagon wheels sank deep into it, and the horses thrust their huge shoulders taut against their collars.

Mark was not confident enough to want to drive the team under these circumstances, and he stopped at the crest of a hill. Jim came around from behind the wagon. Yellow mud clung to his overalls to well above his knees.

"You better drive, Jim," Mark said to him.

From the crest of the hill the boy looked out through the pouring rain. Through that grey and rainy afternoon as Mark Cullen sat hunched under the improvised top of a hay wagon, he looked out over Scatterfield. It lay stretching its ugly face over five square miles. It was like a face blotched and scarred with ulcers. That was the way it looked from the hilltop. It looked worse when they really got into it. The horses had to pull, and pull hard, downhill. Now that the footing was more precarious, the cow decided that she would walk without the aid of the lash, and Mark crawled under the canvas where he could see and keep the drenching rain from his hide.

The landscape was barren of vegetation, except for tufts of weeds and brown grass that showed up on slopes and hillsides like a moth-eaten beard on the face of an idiot. The houses were mostly hovels and shacks. To the boy it seemed that they could not under any circumstances be dignified by the name of home. They leaned and tipped this

way and that, each with a rickety outhouse standing too close to the back door. From back door
to outhouse planks were strewn through a sea of
yellow mud. In the same fashion boards were
strewn from front door to cinder paths which lined
the muddy streets.

The wagons came in on Delaney Avenue. Later,
Mark learned that it was so named for old John
Delaney, who owned most of Scatterfield. He had
named most of the streets for members of his
family, but when shacks began to accumulate in
the eastern section of town he ran out of names.
Streets on the east side were called "Sunset Drive"
and "Brookside Boulevard" and "Eureka Avenue."

Old John had thought of a host of picturesque
names. He had built every house in Scatterfield,
and he boasted that he could build a good house
in a day. Most of them were built that way. Only
a few houses had plastering and wallpaper. Some
of them were lined inside with tar paper for pro-
tection from chill winter winds. The kitchens
were scarred and poverty-ridden and without covering on the floor. The women were lean and tragic.
They were dirty. They were lined and bent with
toil and childbirth, but they neither wept nor
laughed. They were beyond all emotion.

The horses thrust hard against their collars. The
hames creaked, and their giant muscles rolled under
smooth, sweaty coats. Their legs sank deep into

the thick mud, and they drew forth their feet with a loud, sucking noise. The wheels of the wagon sank nearly to the axle.

Kids began to line the cinder paths to watch the progress of the wagons through the streets. They were dirty and ragged. They shouted rudely and laughed boisterously. Their vocabulary was replete with profanity. As they walked along to keep pace with the wagons the cinder paths seemed to weave under their feet like rubber ice. Yellow clay showed through the paths in places. Slowly, with season after season, the mud was swallowing them up.

The wagons passed John Delaney's grocery store. Some men were sitting under a leaky awning. They watched morosely. Back of the store lay old John's lumber yard, exposed year after year to the wind and rain.

A boy about Mark's age ran out of the lumber yard and came out to the street. He was barefooted, despite the cold and rain. His little face was hard, and he had stored in his cheek a huge chew of tobacco. He stood on the cinder path and squirted a stream of tobacco juice at the spokes of the wagon wheels. He looked up then, and saw Mark crouched beneath the canvas.

"Well, Jesus Christ!" he blurted. "Will you look at that goddam country jake!"

He stood gazing cynically after the wagon but

made no effort to follow. His manner frightened Mark a little, and the boy began to fear that he would not have such an easy time in Scatterfield.

The wagon passed a shack where a woman was driving a skinny cow into a shed in the yard. She held a board in her hand with which she beat the cow's bony rump. She was afflicted with facial paralysis, and her mouth was twisted far to one side. From beneath her ear her crooked mouth moved as she hurled vile curses at her charge. She paused a moment to look at the wagon and then slapped her buttocks and waved. She observed Mark's look of amazement and laughed a shrill and twisted laugh.

On the opposite side of the street stood a small, one-room building which had been painted brown long ago. Now the paint was peeling off in huge rolls, exposing again the yellow, aged boards beneath. A cheap, striped barber sign had been painted over the door frame, and a sign in the window read: BARBER SHOP—HAIR CUT, 15 cents— SHAVE, 10 cents. A man in a dirty white jacket stood at the window. He was smoking a black stogie. He gazed at the wagon steadily with melancholy eyes.

Past the next street intersection and far back from the street stood a long, low, one-story house. A few paces from the house stood an outhouse and woodshed, side by side. Outside the shed door a boy was chopping wood and stacking it in a small pile for immediate use. He did not heed the rain which poured down on his head. Inside the shed door stood a lanky hound dog. It stretched and opened its cavernous mouth in a wide yawn.

The horses splashed on through the mud. The wagon passed a worm-eaten apple orchard on the roll of a little hill. The trees were twisted and unhealthy. Many of them were dead, with half-rotten trunks rooted into the yellow clay.

Beyond the orchard stood a frame school building. It was rickety and seemed ready to collapse. It had not been painted for years and was now a dirty, scaly grey. The yard had been covered with gravel which was slowly sinking into the yellow mud beneath.

It was after school hours, but several ragged boys came out the door. They had evidently been kept after school. The first boy turned abruptly and struck the second on the point of the jaw. They both grappled and fell in the mud and gravel.

They bit and scratched and tore at each other like wild animals. They screamed and cursed. A heavy-jowled and stocky man ran from the schoolhouse and jerked the boys to their feet. He cuffed them severely. They took their cuffing with silent resentment and splashed off through the mud, each on separate ways. The first boy looked back toward the schoolhouse. Observing that the man had disappeared, he shouted to the other.

"I'll git you yet, Cockie, goddam you!" he shouted.

"Like hell you will!" assured the other.

The wagon now passed over an improvised bridge of planks which lay haphazard over a small stream. The stream was swollen to immense proportions. The water was yellow, and it rushed madly. It overflowed its small channel. It came up to the floor of the bridge and tore furiously at the planks. It looked uncertain to cross that bridge, but the other wagons had passed safely over it, and Jim McLain followed. He made it and drew up behind the other wagon, which was stuck in the mud.

The cow, still tethered to the back of the wagon, stood knee-deep in the yellow sea and bawled. She had had no food nor water since morning, and her udder was heavy with milk. Mark had had no food either, but the chew of tobacco had kept down his appetite. He was just beginning to feel a little hungry, and his head ached and throbbed. His muscles were sore. He was miserable.

Ed Dill was driving the wagon in front. He got down and came back.

"Jeeezus!" he growled. "Hain't this fierce, Jim?"

"Sure is," Jim agreed.

"Think I'll let you drive 'em out, Jim," Ed suggested.

"Sure," said Jim. "I'll take 'em out."

Every man who knew Jim knew that he was an expert teamster. Jim knew horses, and he knew how to handle them. Ed wanted Jim to drive him out of trouble. Jim took another chew and climbed on Ed's wagon. He geed and hawed and talked to the horses. He backed and manipulated them and drove them right out of it. Then he came back to his own team.

"There wasn't nothing wrong with them horses except that they was tired," he said to Mark. "Them horses needed a rest."

Now the wagon climbed a long, steep hill where the horses had to dig frantically for solid footing. At the top there was less mud. From there on they didn't have to labor so hard.

At his left Mark got his first look at the Scatterfield graveyard. It was pretty well filled with graves, but there were only a few headstones. There had been some effort to keep grass on the place, but yellow clay showed through in great spots. It was a bleak-looking place and not calculated to make Mark want to die very soon.

Several of the graves were marked with implements of labor, indicating the occupations in which the dead men had engaged. Thus, heavy anvils and brake wheels and iron levers pressed down the heads of tired workers. The graveyard was fenced in at the back, where it ended at the crest of a hill.

Down through the valley rushed the brook, and far across to the opposite hillside Mark could see great patches of scrub pine against the facing of a cliff. Tipped precariously at the top stood a shack with smoke rolling from its tin chimney. A man stood before the door with his hands thrust deep in his pockets.

The wagons ahead got stuck three more times before Mark got to his new home. Jim's wagon got stuck once, but it didn't take him long to pull out. You couldn't fool Jim with a team in any kind of mud. Mark knew that.

Shortly before they reached their destination Mark led the cow over the cinder path. He was so tired that the path and street bobbed up and down with every step he took. A great pain shot through his back. He had never been so tired before in his life—but he always knew that feeling when it came to him again. He always thought of the cinder path—and of Scatterfield.

The house was snug. It was snug for a house in Scatterfield. It had three rooms downstairs and two up. Mark was to have a little room of his own with a coal stove for heating. He reflected at once that he could go there and read on cold winter nights. It had a sickly looking lawn—just patches of grass with earth showing through like ulcers. But there was a picket fence before the house. It was the only picket fence in Scatterfield.

Mark knew that his father would bring out the lawn. He would scatter chicken manure over it until it looked and smelled like a chicken yard. But a little later you would see grass spring out of it.

There was a good, tight, weather-sheeted barn and chicken house. Michael always had to have something to farm with—something must always be about his place to remind him of the country. The more he had to work to produce garden truck the more it pleased him. Poor soil tested his skill and knowledge, and he liked the contest.

Michael paid the teamsters for two days' work, for they would not want to work their teams next day. They wouldn't be home until midnight. Mark knew Jim McLain wouldn't work his team next day, but he was uncertain about Ed Dill and the other man, whom he did not know. Michael fed their horses from the supply of hay and corn he had stored in his new barn.

While Judy directed the work, the teamsters set up the stoves. They put up the kitchen coal range first, and Judy boiled coffee.

When she learned about Mark's trying adventure, she had his bed put up.

"You'll have to take a hot foot bath and castor

oil," she told him. "We don't want you to catch
pneumonia. I'll have Pop do the chores."

Mark was willing to take anything to get out
of the chores, and he went through with the whole
ritual. Then he went to bed.

The whole day flooded into his mind like a
nightmare. He thought about the swollen, yellow
stream and the sticky mud. He remembered the
dirty kids. They were so dirty that he expected
scales to drop off them. He shuddered when he
thought of the old woman with a crooked mouth.
And as he thought of the graveyard he remembered
that he didn't want to die of pneumonia.

And while thinking he grew more apprehensive
about the town. He felt certain he could never
like such kids. But later, when he learned more
of the hardness of their lives and of the beatings
they took from their old men and of the times
they went hungry, he liked them very much. Later, he fought with them and for them. He learned
to pilfer, to smoke cigarets, and to tell dirty stories.

In those seasons that followed he learned to wait
for the drunken men who came home from their
work in the city on Saturday nights. Each morning
they rode to their work in the city on rickety street-
cars that leaped and bounded and jumped over uncertain rails. Each day they made such a pilgrimage,
and on Saturdays they came back late at night to

stumble with drunken feet over Scatterfield's cinder paths.

Some of them beat their wives and kids. And
Mark stood outside their hovels with Nutsie and
Cockie and Soap Dodger and Wickie. With them
he listened to the uproar. They heard dishes crash
against walls and women wail. They heard gruff
voices cursing. The boys outside always laughed.
They knew their beatings, too.

But that all came long after—when Mark had
learned something of men and their toil and how
toil often warps lives. That night he lay in a half-
sleep with an aching, painful body. And he thought
of Jim McLain sitting in a hunched position on his
hay wagon. Jim McLain with his hardened teamster hands and a great work hump on his back—
driving a fine team through the dark night....

Now it was Monday morning, and very soon
now Mark Cullen would be going to school. And
he lay in bed thinking about that new school—
that Scatterfield school. Sleep hadn't deserted him
entirely, but just the same his nerves were beginning to tingle with apprehension. The circumstances didn't appear to be promising, and a sense
of fear and loneliness began to possess him.

And there were little noises creeping into his
room, nudging the lazy silence and sweeping sleep
from his eyes. At intervals he could hear the faint

tinkle and clatter of dishes from the kitchen below where his mother was preparing breakfast. The savory odor of fried ham came floating into the room to sharpen his senses a little more. He would soon be awake.

All the noises coming into the room were very faint and far away. Michael and Judy were talking, but Mark couldn't distinguish one word from another. Just a low, droning mumble of words, interrupted now and then by the tinkle of dishes and silverware being placed on the table.

Little puny outdoor noises came sifting through the windowpane, too, and tumbled lazily about the room. It was hard to tell what they were. Just a jumble of sounds coming faintly into him—waking him up.

When someone walked by on the cinder path before the house he could tell what that sound was. He could tell footsteps by the even crunch, crunch of the cinders. And he could tell if the person were hurrying—if maybe he were late to work, or if he were just strolling along and didn't care.

Judy had called the boy once, and now he was resting in the luxurious certainty that he would be called again. It was pleasant to lie there and wait to be called. It wasn't long. She called again.

"You'll be late to school, boy," she said.

Years later it was the same voice
and an older face. Only one word
was changed. "You'll be late to
work. . . . "

"All right, Mom," he said lazily.

Then Mark got up and looked out the window.
His window faced the east, and he could see a
long way from it. He could see the three mud-
filled streets beyond, and a little to the right he
could see one corner of the graveyard. Where the
land dropped sharply into the deep ravine he could
see the swollen brook lashing madly through its
crooked channel like a wounded serpent.

A single tree, gaunt and naked, stood at the top
of the hill beyond. The earth had slipped from
beneath half its roots so that it leaned helplessly
toward the gorge below. Its gnarled and twisted
roots stuck forth like a multitude of supplicating
arms. They cast lacelike shadows over the yellow
facing of the cliff. Below the cliff a few scrub
pines thrust themselves feebly upward. The green
of them stood out vividly against patches of rusted
grass that lay about like worn and threadbare
carpets.

It had rained almost continually over the week
end, but now the big, red sun was creeping slowly
up into a clear, blue sky. The streets were thick
with mud, and the heavy wagon tracks through

them looked like wrinkles in a face that is yellow with age.

The hovels and shacks strewn about slopes and hillsides were like an army of aged beggars squatting in postures of utter dejection. They were careless of wind and rain and sunshine alike. The town didn't look so bleak and grey now. But it looked dreary.

Mark stood there silently until he began to feel cold. And then he started to dress. It would probably be cold out of doors, he thought. The bright sun looked warm, but it was probably a fooler.

He turned again to the window to watch a man who had just come from an outhouse across the street. The fellow stood on a row of planks which led through a sea of mud to his kitchen door. He looped his suspenders carefully over his shoulders and adjusted his trousers. Then he thrust his hands in his pockets and contemplated the blue sky overhead. He appraised it carefully and then walked toward the house.

A woman came out and threw dishwater into the yard, and a boy came from the front door with schoolbooks strapped at the end of a shinny club. He carried the club over his shoulder like a musket. Mark remembered that he had better hurry. He finished dressing and went downstairs.

When he sat down at the table for breakfast,

Michael launched into a long lecture. Mark knew that was coming.

Michael said that this was a new school. He was district superintendent. Mark must conduct himself in a gentlemanly fashion and not put him to embarrassment. He described at length the rewards of an education, which seemed to be pretty great if you had to struggle for it.

Michael had been a poor boy and had had to put forth such a struggle. He did not regret it. His home had been a very humble one, and he had received no encouragement. Mark's opportunities, said Michael, were much greater than his father had ever had. Mark must exercise care and not get into bad company. Bad company, it seemed, was a snare which tripped up many a boy and sent him on the road to an evil life.

Mark answered yeah, yeah, to all the lecture, wishing all the while that Michael would stop. There was nothing new in it. The boy had heard it all a thousand times.

When Michael spoke that way his face assumed an expression of great earnestness. Words fell from his lips with faltering emphasis. Sometimes he halted a moment while his methodical brain groped for the exact word. When he did this his lips trembled. His lips tried vainly to speak the word which his mind had not yet produced. Sometimes he would pick with nervous fingers at a mole on the

end of his nose. His effort always appeared labo-
rious. His face drew up into a mass of wrinkles,
and he scowled fiercely.

But Mark was now more interested in the bright
shaft of sunlight coming in at the window to
spread itself on the tablecoth. Judy sat quietly and
studied the little particles of dust which rolled
languidly through the light.

Michael got up, finally, and said: "I'll do the
chores this morning, Mark. Then I'll have to hitch
up and drive to Slatesville to visit a school."

He said it benevolently, like he wanted to be
helpful. But Mark had heard his mother arrang-
ing that part of the program the night before.
She smiled a little—smiled to herself.

"Yeah," said Mark. "It's gettin' kind of late."

"Mr. Light is your regular teacher," Michael
went on. "But he won't be at school today. He's
sick again. Got a woman substitute. Her name is
Deems. See that you don't give her any trouble."

"Uh-huh," Mark answered.

Then he started to strap up his books. Judy followed the boy to the front room. The milk buckets
rattled in the kitchen. Mark put on his sweater
and cap. Judy put her arm about his shoulder and
walked with him to the door.

"You be careful today, son," she said softly. And
the old frightened look was in her face. "You be
a good boy."

"Yeah," Mark said. "All right. I will."

At the front gate Mark observed a boy walking toward him. Mark walked slowly, hoping that the kid would catch up. Maybe he could learn something about the school—about the other kids.

At the Delaney Avenue hill the boy walked past Mark, and he saw that the other was dirty and had little eyes set between red, swollen lids. He wore no hat, and his hair was matted and twisted like a crow's nest. You could tell he hadn't bothered to comb it.

His teeth protruded, and from one corner of his mouth a scabby patch ascended nearly half his cheek. It didn't look like an injury. It looked like some sort of skin disease.

"Goin' to school?" inquired Mark in his very pleasantest manner.

And that ragged scamp turned his head away and quickened his stride. He spit through his protruding teeth.

"Tzzzit!"

"You s'pose I'm out walkin' fer my health or somethin'? Where d'ya s'pose I'm goin'?"

He scowled and dug his worn shoes into the cinders angrily. He hurried on.

To Hell with you, thought Mark Cullen—but he thought it just to keep his courage up. His heart beat fast, and he walked slowly on.

For a moment he stopped and looked down the

hill before him—into the valley where Delaney Avenue crossed the stream. A group of boys stood on the edge of the rickety bridge hurling stones into the torrent beneath them.

A little farther on stood the school building. Splotched and scarred, it reminded Mark of a scaly monster asleep in the sun.

From all the streets in every direction came swarms of dirty kids, trudging slowly toward the school, with books and dinner pails in their hands. Kids walked in the yard in groups. Some were at play, and they shouted boisterously. Their thin, faraway voices came up to Mark almost softly.

It was like watching some puzzling sort of theatrical production where a great many actors are on the stage at once—a great many actors who go through all sorts of queer antics which seem to have no particular meaning. A queer sort of play that you can't understand at all.

The sun was bright, but it wasn't warm. There was a stiff, hungry breeze. It penetrated Mark's clothing and gnawed into his skin. It raised tiny waves on puddles of water in the street. Mark thought they looked like goose-pimples. He walked on, thinking hard.

It would have been a great day to walk in the woods far back of the old house, he thought. He would have walked in the woods and listened to the twigs and dead leaves crashing beneath his feet. Alone. The wind would have rustled through the leaves—whispering in a melancholy voice and every once in a while would snap them petulantly against the trunks of trees.

Maybe Mark would have felt a little bit sad—but not too sad. Just pleasant—sort of. Then, if he had wanted to, he might gather leaves and pile them into a heap; bury himself in them and lie there and get warm. The wind would moan and sigh through the tall, bare branches of trees, and there Mark Cullen would be in a nest of leaves getting warm. He would probably feel sad—but not too sad.

But he was close to the bridge now, and had to stop thinking about the woods. The boys standing there had stopped talking among themselves and stood watching him morosely. The one who had passed Mark on the hill had now joined the others, and he stood a little to the front.

Mark was a little apprehensive now. He was almost certain they would start a fight, and he supposed they could trim him hands down. They looked like they could do a good job of it. With a sense of quivering about the stomach and with heart pounding in his breast, Mark Cullen determined to give what he could and to take it.

The cinder path divided itself at the bridge where a few cinders had been flung across the planks by hurrying feet. Among the group standing there was the blond-headed boy who had spit tobacco juice through the spokes of the wagon wheels the day Mark came into Scatterfield. He was still barefooted and was chewing vigorously on a huge cud of tobacco. At intervals he turned to squirt a stream of amber juice into the brook where the mad rushing water hurried it away to dissolution. He looked pretty expert at chewing tobacco. Mark knew it took long practice to send such a stream of spittle through the air.

Beside him stood a boy who looked like a half-wit because of his dull eyes and the manner in which his mouth hung open. Mark could see his long, red tongue lying idly between his teeth. And there was another lad who was so tall and thin and stooped that he resembled a drooping cornstalk. His face was haggard, and his eyes seemed old and wise. They were all ragged.

They were silent as Mark walked across the bridge. The water beneath sprayed and fumed and roared so that his footsteps were lost in confusion. Mark had retreated from them some distance when their voices resumed. There was a snicker then, and a laugh that cut like a knife. Mark could feel their eyes and guess their remarks.

He had gone a short distance when the school bell rang. It wasn't a real school bell; just a hand bell that a teacher jangled from the window.

Lagging feet now broke into a hurrying run,

and two long queues began to form before the door. One line was made up of smaller children who would go into the little room. Mark joined the larger kids.

Then, from inside the building, an old piano, badly out of tune, struck up a chord, and the kids began to march in. The chord was "Chop Sticks," and no one could really march to it. The kids' feet didn't go chump! chump! chump! chump! like feet do in a genuine march. Instead the feet struck stairs and hallway inside at uneven intervals, and the sounds were caught up in a multitude of mad, dancing echoes. The echoes dodged and leaped from wall to wall. The notes from the piano were hurled forth insistently to drop to the floor in despair and confusion. Still other notes bravely followed—striving vainly to collect these noises into a powerful and rhythmic beat.

Mark took one last longing glance at the bright out of doors before the doorway swallowed him. In a field beyond the schoolhouse lay a large water pond, its yellow belly stretched out languidly in the sunlight. Two naked trees, staunch and straight, stood at the far end of it—like sentinels guarding its slumber. Then the doorway closed about him.

Miss Deems, the substitute teacher, stood at the top of a short flight of stairs inside and between the two lines of marching pupils. She had a stern, white face—rather pinched features, they were—and without humor. She wore a white waist with huge, puffy sleeves. It tapered into a thin, corseted waistline where it connected with a long, black, plaited skirt. In her hand she held a rule which she swung back and forth after the manner of an orchestra leader. This gesture was not in time with the music or the pounding feet, so that it looked gravely idiotic.

Behind her sat a fat girl at the piano. Her chubby fingers sought the keys mechanically, and in them was no sense of rhythm or time. She sat like an automaton, plunking the keys with fat fingers—lazy, effortless fingers that had learned the keyboard. She looked with dull, unseeing eyes into the music board where her heavy reflection lay, hugely magnified. Her bulky buttocks rolled helplessly over the piano stool like two soft, bulging pillows.

Mark marched in the door, and a few stragglers followed. Then the music stopped, and its echo, mingling with others, tumbled about in the air for a moment, drifted languidly down the long corridor, stirred again ever so lazily, and dropped into weary silence.

Inside the room there was the sound of many shuffling feet, clattering slates, rustling papers, and of pencils noisily rattling into holders at the tops of desks. Then the door closed noiselessly behind the teacher and Margaret Castell, the fat girl who had played the piano. The latter waddled slowly to a seat near the front and sat down. It creaked ominously under her weight.

There were hurried whispers and snickers. Miss Deems walked across the room and placed her hand on her desk. She looked about her with an air of stern authority.

"Silence, please!" she said commandingly.

A complete and deadening silence followed.

Mark looked about him. There was an old jacketed stove in the center of the room, and the ancient floor beneath it sagged. The flooring was pine and the reinforcement beneath it so frail that it weaved perilously under pounding feet.

The stove rested on a square of tin which was cluttered with bits of coal. A fine coating of grey ashes lay strewn from the fire pot across the floor, like drool from an ancient chin. The stovepipe climbed straight to the ceiling, where it stretched itself like a long snake to the far corner of the room to join the chimney.

The room was large, with windows at the side and back. From the side window Mark could see the Delaney Avenue hill. He could see people spring into view at the crest and drop slowly from sight beneath the window ledge. The walls of the room were painted a dead grey, so that it always seemed dark, even on a bright day.

Mark had taken a seat between a girl and the blond-headed boy. It was back of the stove, where he would not always be in view of the teacher. Two legs of his desk had been jerked loose from the floor and could be moved about when the seat attached to it was vacant.

The top of the desk was carved with initials and figures. There were dates and meaningless lines and crevices and holes—just hacked and chipped out with no purpose in view. It was as rough as a washboard. One of the carved symbols startled Mark a little, and he wondered about it. He had never seen such a figure carved in a school desk. It was the kind you sometimes see in school outhouses.

The girl on his left was frail and slender, with big, red hands. Her face was lean and pinched, which caused her large eyes to look even larger. Beneath her eyes were deep, velvety patches of dark flesh. Her dress was faded, and in the upper sleeve there was a large tear. Her bony shoulder stuck through it like the blade of a jackknife.

Miss Deems cleared her throat auspiciously.

"Now, we'll all bow our heads and repeat the Lord's Prayer," she announced.

She bowed her own head and launched into it. A piping chorus of voices joined hers. The girl by Mark's side clasped her bony red hands and prayed fervently—asking God not to forget her daily bread. Two short braids of greasy hair dropped over her shoulder. She looked wistful.

But the blond-headed boy wasn't praying. He pulled a package of scrap tobacco from his pocket and extracted several flakes. With them he lined his lower lip. Then he looked at Mark and half extended the package, raising his eyebrows in an offering gesture. Mark shook his head. Then the boy leaned toward him and whispered.

"What's your name?"

"Mark Cullen."

"Hain't you the superintendent's kid?"

The question disturbed Mark. It was, he knew, a situation difficult to overcome among kids—this being the superintendent's kid. Mark had always to show the other kids that it didn't make any difference and that he never squealed.

"Yeah," he said finally. "What's your name?"

"Soapy," grinned the boy. "Soap Dodger Pendleton. They call me that on the account that I don't never wash myself."

That wasn't hard for Mark to believe. The kid had a ring of dirt around his neck, and his hands were filthy.

Soapy began to fashion paper wads with rolled bits of paper. He placed them in a rubber band looped about his thumb and forefinger and shot across the room. He aimed at a boy toward the front. The boy was more neatly attired than anyone else in the room. Soapy shot several times and missed, but the sound of the wads striking the wall was lost in mumbling voices. Soapy turned again to Mark.

"That there is Harold Knowles," he ventured, pointing toward his target. "His old man is president of the school board. He's always a teacher's pet. He knows too damn much. I give him a trimmin' once, an' his old man was goin' ta have me sent to the Reform Farm. But he didn't git by with it."

Droning voices continued. When Mark next glanced at the girl he found that she was looking at him. She concealed her lower lip with her upper teeth in a gesture of reproof. Soapy saw her, too. He pointed to her.

"She'll tell on us fer talkin'," he whispered. "Her name is Ellen Smathers, an' she's a snitch."

When the prayer ended Ellen was immediately in a frenzy of eagerness. She tossed her red hand about in the air so frantically that it resembled a flapping flag in a stiff breeze.

"What is it?" said Miss Deems.

"Them two boys was whisperin' while we was havin' prayer," she announced modestly.

Her announcement was made with the air of one who reveals to the world a terrible truth.

Miss Deems folded her arms. She looked disdainful. Then she walked slowly down the aisle and stood between the two boys, looking first at one and then the other.

Soapy opened his tablet, took up a pencil, and dipped it between his moist lips. He placed the pencil against the paper but didn't write anything. He just held the point there without moving it.

"It seems to me that boys your age ought to have more respect for such things," she said coldly. "What do you think about it, Olin?"

She looked at Soapy, and Mark judged Olin must be his real name.

"Yes'm," Soapy agreed mildly.

"And you, young man," she went on, turning to Mark. "You are a new pupil, and you mustn't think you can come into this school and have things your own way. These boys and girls know that I'll not stand for nonsense. What is your name?"

"Mark Cullen."

"Oh," she said, growing a little mellow. "You're the superintendent's boy. Well, don't you think you ought to set an example for the other children? You ought to be a gentleman, you know.

"I don't think your father would want to hear that you have been talking during prayer, do you?" she continued.

"No'm," said Mark, embarrassed by her moralizing.

"Well—ah—let's not do it again," she concluded mildly.

Then, turning her attention to Mark entirely, she spoke in a low voice.

"You haven't had an assignment yet, and I shan't expect you to recite this morning. Study the afternoon lesson now, and you can recite then."

She leaned over Mark's desk and began to fumble with his books, pointing out the lesson in History and Arithmetic and Spelling. There was a faint odor of powder and traces of perfume about her person which pleased the boy's senses. Her hands were clean and white, and her fingernails were trimmed and delicately curved. He liked that part of her, but she was stern and didn't seem to know how to smile.

When she returned to the front of the room, Soapy resumed his whispered conversation.

"I know'd she would tell," he said. "I know'd that damned little snot would tell. That's what she's back here for. Old Man Light put 'er back here to watch me. She's meaner than cow dirt. She sure is!"

Then he went on explaining who various persons were in the room. Miss Deems bent over her desk, studying the roll; checking those present and absent. Soapy pointed to the half-wit who sat a few seats toward the front and in the next aisle.

"That there is Wickie Winters," he explained.

"He don't know very much, but he's a good guy."

Pointing to the scabby-faced kid, now plucking idly at the diseased patch of flesh about his mouth, Soapy continued.

"That's Scrappy Dolan, and he's no damn good. We don't allow him to run in our gang. I've trimmed him, too. But Cockie Werner up yonder. He runs around with us. He's a good guy. He's good at ketchin' frogs. Nutsie Doane is in our gang, but he's a Catholic an' goes to school in the city, 'cause they hain't no Catholic schools in Scatterfield."

And he rambled on and on, giving Mark many bits of valuable information which he needed to adjust himself to new circumstances.

Finally the class got into recitation, and Mark settled himself to study. Time was an old man that day, groping his blind way through a wilderness. It seemed an eternity until recess.

At noon Soapy and Scrappy chose up sides for a game of shinny. Mark was Soapy's first choice. Mark was pleased. It showed that Soapy was willing to give a fellow a chance. When Soapy asked him where he wanted to play, Mark said he could shinny off pretty well, and Soapy said to try it.

The kids played in a big field back of the school-house. It was high ground and not very muddy. The mud was stiff and didn't cling to the shoes.

Mark could see the water pond from the field,

and Soapy said that the gang skated there in winter
—those who had skates, he added. Soapy said he
had a pair of skates, though. He said he stole them
from the back room of John Delaney's grocery
store. He mentioned it very casually and added
that he would try to get Mark a pair in the same
place later on.

There are some days that slip clear out of the
memory after they have been spent. And there
are days that come back to you to cry in a thin,
small voice—to plead before the vaults of memory
for admittance. Still others there are which stand
out in vivid detail. They lie upon the walls of the
mind like a picture chiseled into stone.

In such a picture you can see the faces of people
you have known far back in time—you can see
them clearly. The lines, the crevices, the eyes, the
hair. By closing your eyes you can call forth the
whole scene. And if you are in a quiet room you
may hear them speak; recognizing the queer individual tones and inflections belonging to each voice.

Then again, in fancy, you can stand before a
window and look out of it. A window in a schoolroom—perhaps—a schoolroom that does not exist
any more, except in that queer crevice in the mind.

And from that window you can see a whole town
stretched before you. A town of desolate and haphazard houses sprawled brazenly over slopes and

hillsides. The hills are yellow clay, and because the sun is shining the color cuts sharply into the mind. Between the hills are valleys and lowlands. Some of them are jagged, like deep scars; and long, black shadows lie across them, hurled from the hills above.

And you can see the yellow, muddy streets winding and intersecting—tracing their purposeless way through the barren countryside. Perhaps through one of them a team of horses drags a wagon loaded with lumber. From your faraway lookout you cannot hear the shouting teamster, the jangling chains on the harness, or the rattling wheels of the wagon. But you can see how the horses lean forward and struggle through the mud. You can see all of it, but you must guess the sound. And you wonder about life and why so much of it escapes you. It is a meaningless pantomime.

Days like this are long days. They are long because you are so conscious of reality. Time stretches itself so far that you catch a fleeting glimpse of eternity.

A boy's first day in a strange school he never forgets. Not so long as the fabric of his mind holds together. When he becomes a man he will remark it more clearly than his daily life. Especially he will remember it if he comes from a peaceful country home to live in a town of rattly shacks standing over barren hills. Hills of hungry, yellow mud, eager to devour the world. Such a contrast is like dreaming that life is a thing of rare beauty. Then to come forth from the dream and find life standing before you—raw and bleeding, its sullen eyes fastened upon you and its jaw hanging limp with despair.

After school Soapy walked home with Mark, eager to interpret the town and its people. Why he did this Mark never knew. For Soap Dodger Pendleton was a mean kid and was rarely decent to strangers. He delighted in mean tricks and practical jokes. And this was not from a distorted sense of humor, but from an inbred notion that he must always get the other guy first. Years later Mark Cullen wondered why Soapy was good to him from the start—why Soapy never made him a target for his tricks. But Mark Cullen was never put in that position.

After Mark finished his chores that night he crawled into the hayloft and stayed there a long time. He was conscious of noise and its nearness and at the same time felt very far away. He called into his mind the day's happenings—not in words but in pictures.

A boy never has words for things that happen to him. He only feels keenly, but he cannot translate that feeling. His words are a stammering evasion. So Mark lay there in the soft hay, breathing its stale fragrance, and calling forth the day just spent. Calling it forth without words. Watching long, golden lances of sunlight filter through cracks in the barn to cut into heaps and mounds of hay. Feeling that he had departed the world awhile so that he might watch it casually.

At the supper table Judy asked the boy how he got along in school.

"All right," Mark answered. And he ate a long while, still thinking about it. Then he communicated to her a fragment.

"There is a kid in school, Mom, that they call Soap Dodger," he said, "because he is awful dirty an' don't never wash hisself. He's just as dirty an' ornery as he can be. But he's an awful good fellow. He sure is!"

"Uh-huh," answered Judy quietly.

"You be careful about getting in with boys like that," howled Michael, waving his knife menacingly. "And watch your grammar. It sounds like the devil!"

Mark didn't say any more. It didn't appear to be of any use to talk.

Time passed on its relentless way, and Mark grew accustomed to his new home. He came, indeed, to feel himself a part of Scatterfield. It wasn't easy at first, but time will always do that for you—wherever you may go.

Everything here was a great deal different than

the old house and its easy country life. Mark
Cullen had never known anything like this. The
kids were different, too. For a long while he wondered why people bothered to live in such a desolate place when there were so many habitable spots
in the world. When he grew older he thought
about it in a more logical way. He learned that
there are many Scatterfields in the world for work-
worn men and their broods of children.

Old John Delaney knew this, too. His shrewd
eyes peered inquiringly into the necessities of
workers, and his ballyhoo drew workers to his town.
From his inheritance of many acres of worthless
soil he built his rattly town and filled his purse.

At the far end of Scatterfield in a vacant field
an old sign still stood. It bore a worn and weather-
beaten admonition to be thrifty; buy a lot; own
your own home. The workingman's paradise, it
continued, a small down payment and the balance
in easy terms. But it didn't continue far enough.
It did not reveal that if you were thrown out of
work or had a lean year Old John would pocket
what you had paid and repossess your home as well.
This often happened.

There were more kids in Scatterfield than anything else—or so it seemed to Mark. They were a
ragged and hungry-looking community in themselves. They never played much. They had never
learned about play of the imaginative sort. The

struggle for existence affected all of them. If you lived there the facts of life soon merged themselves with you.

The graves in the Scatterfield graveyard housed many remnants of lives half lived and lives that had scarcely started. Some there were, buried in the dank graves, who had never lived at all.

In the wail of a new-born infant it seemed that you could detect a first cry of protest. But as the young one matured the cry became feeble and half-hearted. It settled into a grim acceptance of things as they are. A good many of them learned soon enough the meaning of hunger and cold. Soapy told Mark that when Cockie Werner was little more than a baby his old man would silence his wails by stuffing a pillow over his face until he was nearly strangled. There were nine other kids besides Cockie. Too many yammering kids.

In the Scatterfield gang Mark soon learned that it was an evidence of weakness to cry about misfortune. If nature herself perpetrated the damage you took your medicine silently. But if some person played you a dirty trick it was a good thing to get even. You got even doubly, if you could. When successful in your attempt you laughed at the other person—he got what was coming to him.

Mark learned these things as soon as possible. Often he pretended to knowledge he did not possess. He was grateful to Soapy for befriending him.

On Soapy's recommendation the rest of the gang soon accepted him as a full-fledged member. In return for their confidence Mark was fiercely loyal to them and hated unreasonably everyone and everything they hated. At first he thought them strange, but not for long.

Saturday was the gang's day, and they spent it in a way that would be fun and would prove a little practical—maybe. They raked through junk-ridden alleys and pawed over the town dump, eager to find something to convert into cash.

Sometimes Soap Dodger pilfered junk from his old man, who was a junk peddler. Then some member of the gang would re-sell it to the old man. The proceeds were divided among the group. This didn't hurt Soapy's conscience in the least. Old Dick Pendleton often laid a heavy fist on Soapy's jaw. When Soapy swiped from him successfully, the old man got a portion of what was coming to him. Soapy considered him a natural enemy.

Very often the gang filched provisions from old Delaney's grocery store. The kids always entered the place when Lovett Smollett, the grocery boy, was tending store alone. All the gang, save Soapy, gathered about Lovett so that he couldn't watch. Then Soapy would get into the tobacco case. He picked up everything he found lying loose. Lovett knew what the kids were about, but he didn't care.

He didn't want to appear to know. All the kids
agreed that it was all right to do this. Everybody
knew that Old John was a thief in his own right.

Soapy said a fellow had to have guts, and Mark
learned what he meant one Saturday.

The gang had gone down to Yellow Creek to
spear fish. The autumn rains had swollen the creek
until it had overflowed miles and miles of the mud
flats along its bank. When it receded into its narrow channel it left great, shallow ponds through
the fields. The ponds were full of fish. Each boy
had fashioned a spear by pounding a nail into the
end of a broom handle and filing the head into a
sharp, needlelike point.

They had killed a huge mess of fish—enough for
their noon meal and a mess for each boy to take
home.

Wickie Winters, the half-wit, was cleaning them.
Soapy explained that Wickie always cleaned the
fish because he liked to cut into things. He liked
to see blood. Wickie's mad little eyes sparkled as
he ripped open their bellies with a jackknife. He
gutted them with clumsy finger, pawing through
the entrails hungrily before tossing them away.
Sometimes his tongue lolled out, and he panted
hoarsely. He frightened Mark until he got to know
about him.

In a little while Nutsie Doane and Cockie
Werner got into a fight about which one was to

have a big bass that Cockie had speared. Nutsie said it was his because he had killed more fish and they were evenly divided. Cockie had all the best of it. He was larger. He mauled Nutsie.

Soapy and Mark watched them indifferently. It wasn't serious. Some of the kids were always in a fight. Wickie was enthusiastic. He danced wildly about, making hoarse little noises deep in his throat.

When Nutsie saw that he had lost he began to laugh to show that it was all in fun. He jumped up and ran for a tree. Cockie followed, cursing.

Nutsie skinned up a tree along the creek bank. His movements were quick. Cockie was more awkward. He crawled slowly, painfully after. Nutsie crawled out on a frail little limb about fifteen feet above ground. It was too frail to hold them both, and Cockie selected a larger one where he could reach and shake the other.

"Git down, Nutsie, goddam you!" he howled. "Git down or I'll shake you down!"

"Go to Hell!" howled Nutsie, feeling safe in his retreat.

Cockie shook the limb furiously. Nutsie, clutching the limb with arms and legs, bobbed about like a rat in the mouth of a terrier.

"Come on, git down!" Cockie insisted.

And then Nutsie got down. The limb cracked and broke clean. The boy went hurtling down

through the air with arms and legs flapping
helplessly.

He struck the ground with a deep, piglike grunt.
He sat up and looked at his forearm where the
sleeve was rolled to the elbow and caked with mud.
A small sliver of bone stuck through the dirty
flesh.

He sat very silently, looking at the bit of bone
with a little trickle of blood slowly creeping down
its bleached whiteness. On the creek bank with
legs spread wide and buttocks in a puddle of water
Nutsie sat with big, dumb eyes fastened on the
limp hand and piece of bone. His sallow face
turned green. Cockie wriggled down the tree.

"Jesus Christ, Nutsie!" he said. "I never meant
to do it."

Nutsie's eyes blinked. He swallowed hard and
said nothing. Mark ripped up his shirt, and Soapy
helped bandage the arm tightly. Wickie whined.
The broken ends of the bones scraped together
audibly when the bandage was placed about the
arm. Nutsie clenched his teeth and sat very still.

"Git some bark, Cockie," Nutsie said. "Like a
splint."

With two long strips of bark Soapy and Mark
bound a makeshift splint about the injured arm,
cushioning it with tufts of grass. Then they made
a two-way seat with their hands and started to
carry Nutsie, but after a time he said he could

walk. It was four miles to Dr. Clarke's office. They carried him part of the way and helped him over fences.

When the doctor set the arm the ligaments had swollen. It took about all his strength to pull the bones together. Nutsie cursed several times but finally closed his lips tightly. He compressed them until they were thin, white, bloodless lines. He made little noises through his nose as his breath broke through in gasps.

On the way home Nutsie kept saying he hoped his old man wasn't drunk. But when he got there he found out soon enough that he was. The old man's befuddled and boozy mind didn't grasp the significance of the clean, white bandage and sling. He slapped Nutsie over without ceremony, and when the kid fell the bones were pushed a little out of line. The arm was always crooked after that.

Later on the old man sobered up, and Nutsie, a little feverish, was out of his mind. He squirmed about and cried aloud so that he could be heard a long way.

Bedraggled neighbors came in to offer assistance, but they were more curious than helpful. Soapy and Mark walked over, too. They watched Nutsie's big, melancholy eyes roam about the room, and they could tell he didn't know them.

The old man sat at the foot of the filthy bed with his big, gnarled hand on the boy's knee.

Nutsie's mother stood at the sink washing dishes patiently. She didn't say much to anyone. She wore a dirty grey dress and was barefooted. Her belly bulged beneath the garment. It wouldn't be long before Nutsie would have a new brother— or sister, maybe.

As the lad's eyes swept the room Old Man Doane tried to fix them with his own. His calloused hand kept caressing the kid's knee, and he spoke in a monotone.

"Don't you know me, son? Don't you know me?" he kept saying.

A long time afterward, when the bones had knitted, Nutsie was ashamed of having cried out in pain. But Soapy reassured him.

"You never know'd nothin' about it," Soapy told him. "You done fine, Nutsie."

Long afterward, and at moments when there was nothing especially to do—when the gang sat about a fire, or along the creek bank fishing— Nutsie would roll up his sleeve and look long and silently at his crooked arm. It was bent upward like half a barrel hoop. The fingers were always open and clutching, like a talon.

Often Nutsie looked—with eyes full of wonder. Probably he relived an incident. Probably he thought of his drunken old man slapping him over —making his arm crooked for life.

Autumn deepened, and the days grew shorter and more grey. There were many, many days when the sun didn't show through the heavy sky overhead. Indian summer came, but if you wanted to see its color you had to go to the creek. The bright sun only reflected a cancer yellow in the streets of Scatterfield.

The days in school seemed long, and when Mark Cullen could he spent them dreaming idly. For that boy was never a student. Sometimes he watched people walking up the Delaney Avenue hill and wished that he, too, might be out of his four-walled prison to walk idly about the town. Often, with book open, words before him became a blur, and his mind carried him away. Carried him anywhere and everywhere away from school.

Sometimes, in fancy, he sat by a pool of water, contentedly watching tiny ripples on its surface. The picture was clear and vivid. He wanted to be away to such a place—never to see the school again. Perhaps he could see small leaves bobbing about on the water, and grass along the shore line nodding and waving in the wind.

If, by chance, his mental wanderings carried him through days of imaginary darkness and rain, still would he remove himself far from school. Perhaps he sat in a shack deep in the woods and drenched himself with the comfort of a warm fire.

But always he could look out into the world

through a window. The world forever lay before him; sometimes dark and somber, but always changing.

And in that shack was a door through which he might go out into the world if his choice lay there. Mark Cullen dreamed throughout all his life—he dreamed of being free, and that dream was never half realized, as it is never realized for any man. But Mark firmly resolved that when he was graduated from the eighth grade of the Scatterfield school he would never enter another. He must overcome Michael's protest. This much he knew.

Old Man Light got over his illness and was at last back in school. Mark didn't like him, which was not to the man's discredit. For schoolteachers were jailers to Mark Cullen, and he never liked any of them.

Old Light talked in a droning monotone which frequently made Mark sleepy with its monotony. He was short and stocky, and his personal tastes were fastidious. He was heavily jowled, and the top of his starched collar hid itself in rolls and rolls of fat. His shoes were highly polished and his clothes neatly pressed.

He boarded with Jake Redman on Clara Street and walked a quarter of a mile each morning to school. He walked with a rapid, mincing step. During the rainy season he carried an umbrella and wore a black slicker and overshoes. He kept on the cinder paths as much as possible, but his journey carried him across several muddy streets where his feet sank so deep that mud went over the tops of his overshoes. When he removed them at school a water line of mud showed about his dainty footgear. This he wiped carefully away with a woolen cloth kept in his desk for that purpose.

He did not leave the room at noon, but made his lunch from an orange which he always brought with him each morning.

Soapy warned Mark that the old boy was a mean one; that he knew how to trounce a kid. Soapy had every reason to know.

"Boy, he don't monkey with you," Soapy said. "Sometimes he uses his fist. He has on me already. He's been sick a lot this year, though."

"What's the matter of him?" Mark asked.

"I don't know," Soapy answered. "But whatever it is I wisht the old bastard'd die of it. Goddam him!"

And he whipped Soapy shortly after that—but maybe Soapy deserved part of it, even if he didn't deserve as much as he got.

It was one afternoon—nearly time for school to be out. Harold Knowles had asked Old Light about something in the lesson, and Light had walked back to Harold's desk to explain it. Soapy hated Harold. All the kids hated him, but teachers liked him.

Old Light had his back to Soapy, and when he

leaned over Harold's desk his pants stretched taut over his fat buttocks. They were as tight as a drumhead.

Soapy had several pin javelins hidden in his desk. They were fashioned from matches and pins. He hurled one of them at Harold, but his aim was poor, and the point plopped into Light's backside. It drilled in pretty deep and stuck solid. Old Light leaped straight into the air, reaching toward his backside with thumb and forefinger. On his face was a look of amazement. He howled.

With a scarlet face and eyes squinted in pain he looked toward Soapy. Soapy gulped, grabbed his geography, and began to study in real earnest. The teacher walked toward him.

"Mr. Light," asked Soapy innocently, "what is it year in the jawgraphy as says about the Chicago stockyards—says year that—ah—'bout—ah——"

But Old Light already had him by the scruff of the neck. Only a few kids in the room knew what had happened. Soapy was lifted high in the air and slammed back into the seat. It broke with a loud clatter, and Soapy went straight through it to the floor. Then the old man carried him kicking from the room.

"You can stay up there in the office until after school," the old man bellowed at him. "Then I'll tend to you properly."

Mark waited for Soapy after school. He was

curious to know what else happened. He knew the
old man had locked him in the office. And he
thought, too, that Soapy had already got more
than was coming to him. Soapy was scowling when
he came out the door.

"Did he whale you again?" Mark asked.

"Jeezus!" Soapy answered. "He sure did."

"I thought he licked you enough in the room."

"Well," Soapy explained. "Mebbe he'd have
thought so, too. Only I was locked in, an' I had ta
take a leak. They wasn't no place to do it. I took
a leak in his overshoe. He didn't like it, I guess."

One evening after school Judy sent Mark to
John Delaney's grocery store for something she
had forgot to order in the morning. It was not dark
when he started, but it soon would be. It was the
time of year then when darkness comes early.

Mark didn't hurry. There was no need to. He
just strolled along slowly, taking his time and thinking about the note Mary Hartman had tossed on
his desk that day at school. He had the note in his
pocket, and he fingered it and kicked at the cinders
thoughtfully. He hadn't paid much attention to
Mary before. He hadn't noticed her particularly.
But he thought her nice, now, even if she did have
freckles.

Mary sat back of Mark in school, and she had
flipped the note across his shoulder to land on his

desk. After he had read it and looked back she appeared to be studying. She didn't pretend that she had thrown it.

He couldn't get her to look at him the rest of the day, and after school she ran up Delaney Avenue as fast as she could go. Mark wondered now, if she really liked him. He thought probably she did. She had said that in the note. He had read it so many times that he knew it by heart.

Dear Mark, it read, *I think you are a nice boy and I like you. Do you know that your front teeth are apart and mine are too? Do you know what that means? It means that we are both going to live far from home. Mary.*

It seemed pleasant to have the note in his pocket. Mark remembered now that her teeth were separated a little in front, like his own. She had deep blue eyes and a stubby nose, and her hair was about the color of taffy. She was pretty, he thought. No, she wasn't exactly pretty; just clean-looking and nice. She wore clean gingham aprons that slipped over her dress. Mark liked the blue one. It made her eyes seem more blue.

Perhaps he ought to think her pretty. He wondered what made a person pretty or not pretty. He decided it must be just in a person's mind. If you thought a person pretty—then they were. So he decided that Mary was pretty. Maybe he'd better not write her. But he thought maybe he would.

He passed slowly by the schoolhouse. It was closed and locked. He hated the sight of its ancient siding, its windows like dull eyes and its double center door like an ugly mouth. Still, he was a little anxious to go to school tomorrow. Maybe he would answer Mary's note—if only it weren't for Soapy seeing everything.

He stopped a moment at Clara Street. She lived there. Maybe he'd walk past her house on the way back. Just walk by casually as though he were going somewhere. Not now. It was still too light.

He was about to wonder if he were in love with Mary and then caught himself and debated the use of the word. It seemed a silly word for a boy to use. He felt a little silly using it. Maybe he'd better just tell himself that he *liked* Mary; that he liked her a lot. That's the way he would say it. Nice, he thought. He could have his thoughts to himself. He didn't need to tell anyone—not even Mary.

He walked on. Dusk was creeping stealthily over Scatterfield, and feeble lights began to appear in the dingy houses along Delaney Avenue. The smell of fried suppers permeated the atmosphere.

Oil lamps thrust their pale and sickly light from dirty windows. Shadowy forms moved about inside. Oil lamps always looked doleful—like old,

old men who are sick and refuse to die. A family quarreled noisily somewhere. A large family—all talking at once. A man walked briskly on the other side of the street. Cinders crunched beneath his feet.

Out of a small, boxlike house with a lean-to kitchen came the voice of a woman singing. Flossie Kershner getting supper and singing. Mark knew about Flossie. Soapy had told him. Her husband must have known, too—and didn't care. He was skinny and drooped like an uprooted weed. He had only one eye. The other had an ugly grey splotch throughout the pupil and was sightless. He worked in a factory in the city and walked slowly as though perpetually tired. He wore black work shirts which smelled of sweat. Soapy had told Mark a good deal about Flossie, and Mark had seen some things with his own eyes.

"They hain't enough men and boys in Scatterfield to give her enough," Soapy had said. "She's like to killed her old man. He's glad when someone else does come in. It rests him up."

Until the weather got too cold for it, Flossie always sat on her front steps watching men and boys who passed her door. She devoured them with her greedy, green eyes. She wore loose garments, drawn about her so that they revealed her round hips. Her large breasts sagged heavily. When really bad weather came she would sit inside and look out the window—sit where she could see and be seen.

"When you get a year older," Soapy had said, "she'll be callin' ya in to fix 'er kitchen sink. An' when ya git in there she'll put ya through yer paces. She'll show ya what's what. Maybe she'll do that pretty soon. We're gittin' about right for her."

Mark listened now to her doleful voice—sad and wailing as it rolled out into the dusk. It was the same song she always sang.

> "I'm a broken down man without credit or cash
>   My clothes are all tattered and torn.
> Not a friend have I got in this whole dreary world,
>   Oh, it's better I'd never been born.
>
> "In vain do I seek for employment,
>   Sleeping out on the ground cold and damp,
> I am stared in the face by starvation,
>   Oh, pity the fate of a tramp.
>
> "Last Saturday night on the P and C road,
>   There came a man weary and footsore;
> He spied a box-car standing lone on the track,
>   So he crawled in and closed up the door.
>
> "He had not gone far in that empty box-car,
>   'Til the brakeman came down with a lamp;
> He was hurled from that freight train and killed
>   by the mail;
>   Because he was only a tramp.
>
> "Kind friends I would have you remember,
>   That every poor man's not a tramp;
> There's many a kind heart a-beating,
>   Beneath the torn clothes of a tramp."

As Mark listened to the doleful words repeated over and over he thought of her body. He thought of it with a vague sort of dread. And a queer longing possessed him for only a moment. He felt a little guilty—a little guilty and a little frightened.

With a sense of virtue he thought of Mary Hartman and her clean gingham aprons. Would she ever be like Flossie? He decided she wouldn't. Mary, he assured himself, was a good girl. But he wondered. Mary Hartman was only a little girl; maybe twelve years old; maybe not quite that old.

Pain clutched him. People change when they grow older. Why should they change? Why were there people in the world like Flossie Kershner? Perhaps Mary would change, too. Once, long ago, Flossie had been a little girl, and probably she hadn't thought much about such things then. But certainly Mary would never be like Flossie. Mark decided that he really must like Mary an awful lot.

He passed John Delaney's lumber yard and approached the store. Some men were sitting on bread boxes under the tattered awning. One of them was standing, and Mark could tell that he was Charlie Heston. Their idle talk came to Mark in a muffled jumble of words. Old Charlie Heston was talking very grandly tonight, and making gestures with the eloquence of a king.

Old Charlie was tipsy, and he blathered incessantly. He didn't talk loud. His voice was soft as silk. Everybody liked him whether he was drunk or sober, and the men about the store listened attentively to what he had to say. When Charlie was drunk he used big words, and no one could understand him. His manner was exaggerated.

He spoke very kindly to Mark when he approached the door. Kids always know about people somehow—whether to like them or not. Mark liked Charlie. Everyone called him Charlie.

"Good evening, Mark," he said, very politely. "I was just discussing the Roman Empire. How do you like the Roman Empire by this time?"

The features of the men about the doorway were shadowy in the uncertain light, but Mark could tell that they were grinning amiably.

"I don't know nothin' much 'bout the Roman Empire, Charlie," Mark answered.

"I mean this, my boy," said the old fellow, sweeping his arm in a wide gesture which seemed to indicate everything about him. "I mean this eternal city of ours."

"Oh, you mean Scatterfield."

"Yes, my boy," Charlie went on gravely. "I mean this very city. This symbol of man's unvarying justice and humanity. My boy, you have lived here some time, now. How do you like it? I should be interested to know."

His voice was soft, and his breath smelled of whisky, an odor Mark thought not unpleasant.

"Yes, sir," Mark said. "I guess I like it all right."

"That's right, Mark," said Charlie, placing his hand on the boy's shoulder. "Always be loyal to your kind."

Mark got the groceries for his mother and started back. He felt a little melancholy now; felt like walking alone somewhere. He decided not to walk past Mary's house. He thought, now, that he would go where he couldn't hear voices.

He was thinking of Old Charlie Heston. Old Charlie Heston, drunk, and talking about things people didn't understand. Maybe he didn't understand them himself.

Once Mark had heard him say that he was in Scatterfield so that he might watch the decline of the Roman Empire. Today he had been drinking and talking of the Eternal City. A queer old man —queer—but sympathetic. His hands were loving hands. They touched all things gently. When his arm had been about Mark's shoulder it had been like a benediction.

He would probably continue drinking, Mark thought, until his legs were wobbly. Then his old feet would stagger and stumble. He would go back to his shack across the ravine from the graveyard. His frail old wife would help him into bed. She wouldn't scold him. She'd just help him into bed gently—and say nothing.

Mark walked past Flossie Kershner's house and

turned into Delaney's apple orchard. Flossie wasn't singing now, and Mark reflected that she and her one-eyed husband were eating fried potatoes and drinking buttermilk.

It was dark and gloomy in the orchard. The gnarled and half-rotten trees were like solemn and shadowy wraiths. The soil beneath Mark's feet was soft and sparsely covered with wiry grass. His feet sank into the muck noiselessly. The lights in the houses along Delaney Avenue blinked wanly and bobbed about uncertainly. He moved slowly on, thinking.

He passed over a little knoll and into the gully where Hump Bing's cabin used to stand. Hump was just a legend to Mark. He never had known Hump. He was in the penitentiary, but everyone in Scatterfield said the old man belonged in an insane asylum. He had gone crazy and raped a young woman and then tried to kill John Delaney. He had thought, had Hump, that old age was a disease and that he had caught the disease from Old John. He said he raped the young woman so that she might communicate her youth to him.

Old Charlie Heston said that maybe Hump wasn't so crazy after all. Sanity and insanity are only relative terms, Old Charlie had said. But no one in Scatterfield understood what Charlie meant. They said there was no doubt about Hump. He was plain crazy, they said.

But when Mark got to thinking about Hump he became a little frightened. He had wandered a long way in the darkness and could no longer see the street lights. He got to imagining that Hump had escaped and was out there in the orchard, maybe. His mind kindled with terror which choked out the brooding melancholy thoughts that had possessed him.

Goose flesh came out on his body, and he began to run. He stumbled out through the darkness and over the knoll. He fled like a deer, clutching his packages and breathing hard. The dark forms of trees flitted by him like frightened monsters. A twig cracked loudly beneath his flying feet, and a chill leaped up his spine. His scalp tightened, raising his hair. He plunged madly onward until he brought up in Delaney Avenue, feeling a little ashamed of his cowardice. Then he walked slowly homeward.

That night he lay in bed thinking about Mary. It would be nice, he thought, to have her there in bed with him. Then he thought of his habit of wetting the bed. Try as he would, he could not fully overcome the habit. Well, he told himself, if Mary were there he would just have to stay awake all night. His mind carried the adventure only that far. He permitted himself no greater pleasure than the contemplation of lying in bed with her—feeling the warmth of her body. Besides, it was a little vague beyond that point, anyway.

In the next room he could hear his mother and father preparing for bed. Michael was complaining to Judy about the riffraff Mark was getting in with there in Scatterfield.

"Danged little fool!" Michael was saying. "He hasn't sense enough to choose the proper company. They can lead him around by the end of the nose wherever they want him to go. He never had an ounce of judgment and never will have. Now he wants to quit school and get a job. Danged little bag of bones. What will he ever amount to? Dig in the ditch like the rest of the infernal bunch around here! And he'll never be big enough to stand that!"

Michael, standing in the middle of a chill room and pulling off a long pair of baggy drawers. Michael, picking at the mole of his nose thoughtfully and looking around for his long flannel nightgown. Complaining about the riffraff in Scatterfield. Mark couldn't hear Judy's replies. She always talked very low. But he knew she was attempting to stay his monologue. Mark heard the bed squeak, and as Michael rolled into it his tirade became muffled in the bed clothing. It continued for ten minutes and then dropped into silence. Mark clutched his pillow in a soft caress. He pulled

it close and dived his head into it. Then he fell
asleep.

Deep in the heart of Soap Dodger Pendleton lay
a hidden fear. The most careful study of his er-
ratic activities never revealed it. It was revealed
only occasionally by a remark, or by a quick and
penetrating glance. Soapy was as free as the wind.
And he feared that he might lose that freedom.

Soapy's activities were little concern to his parents. His old man demanded certain work of the
boy. If it was not done, Soapy was soundly beaten.
Old Dick Pendleton penalized his son with a heavy,
gnarled fist. Nothing more.

Soapy went slinking about the town all hours of
the day and night. An expert thief, he took what
he needed from others. He slept often on an improvised bed of rags in the woodshed off the kitchen
door of his home. Sometimes he slept on a cot inside, and sometimes he didn't come home at all.
The latter was true when he feared a beating. His
parents didn't care.

But Soapy was afraid of something. It was a
thing he couldn't strike at—a thing with which he
couldn't even scores. There were forces at work in
that town, demanding that Soapy be sent away to
the Boys' Reform School. Soapy knew about discipline there. He feared four walls. He feared con-

finement. And he feared the strap that went with them.

"I'm the kind they like to git aholt of," he would say, with a quick, frightened glance. This and similar remarks were tossed into casual conversation when a bit of his meanness was a topic for neighborhood discussion.

And you couldn't believe, unless you saw the results of it, that a boy could hate so passionately. The hatred in Soapy's breast was as deep and unswerving as time and eternity. He hated particularly, J. Wellingsford Knowles, president of the school board. He hated old Knowles because the man had been the first to recommend that Soapy be sent away. Knowles later urged that action, frequently.

That same fear settled on Mark Cullen after the events of Halloween. That dark adventure filled Scatterfield with a prolific stench that clung to the town for weeks. The fear it engendered in Mark Cullen stayed with the boy a long time. It never deserted Soapy.

The moon rode high that night when the five members of that Scatterfield gang crept through the dark alleys of that town. Over back fences and through broken fields they moved, as silently as the night itself. Mark was nervous with apprehension, for he had had to go to bed and climb out over the front porch trellis to join the gang.

Each boy, with the exception of Soapy, carried a supply of rotten cabbage and tomatoes. Soapy carried a galvanized bucket and a fire shovel. Ever-widening shafts of light from the windows of J. Wellingsford Knowles' home cut into the darkness, as the kids brought up by his backhouse.

"Come on, Mark," Soapy whispered. "The rest of you guys wait here by the backhouse."

The pair kept well in the shadows until they reached one of the windows. Peering in, they saw him, in starched, white shirt and well-creased trousers, seated before a table. He fingered a water glass half full of red liquid. A glass jug of the stuff sat on the floor beside him.

Mrs. Knowles, small and pale, sat beyond the old man. Occasionally he lifted his glass and gulped with a show of satisfaction. Mrs. Knowles, compressing her lips, glanced at him several times.

"The ol' bastard," Soapy whispered scornfully. "Him a-drinkin' that licker an' talkin' out to other people how bad it is fer ya."

"Mebbe it's jist grape juice," Mark ventured.

"Grape juice, hell!" Soapy said. "Look at that there red nose!"

The nose was pretty red. So were the cheeks. The alcoholic flush was even stealing up in an uneven wave to his partially bald head.

Mark and Soapy crept back to the kids at the

outhouse. Soapy lifted the trap door over the vault, and a horrible stench assailed their nostrils.

"W-h-e-w!" said Nutsie. "J-e-s-u-s, but that stinks!"

"Don't git none of that on ya," Cockie warned.

Wickie giggled and danced.

Soapy, dipping with silent energy, filled the bucket. Mark watched him in silence, thinking that it really was a mean trick to play—even on old Knowles. Soapy carried the bucket to the back porch, emptied it over the steps and floor. Then he smeared some of it on the doorknob.

"Now we'll upset the backhouse," he said, when he got back. "But don't be no damn fools. I want to watch him, so don't run clean away. Circle the barn and hide in them there tall weeds a-crost the road. Let 'em have them cabbages jist as the crapper goes a-flyin'. Now give 'er a heave!"

And they heaved, all five of them, until the outhouse rocked at a perilous balance. With a last shove, it toppled.

"Now throw yer stuff!" howled Soapy.

The backhouse smote the ground with a loud thump, releasing more stench into the otherwise placid night. At the same time an avalanche of rotten vegetables splattered over the house. The thudding footfalls of five kids battered the night. And then all was silence.

Presently the back door opened, flooding the out

of doors with a long trail of light. Old Knowles stood inside for a moment, peering anxiously into the night. Five pairs of eyes watched his every move. He stepped uncertainly to the porch. His foot sank into the soft ooze, and he looked quickly, paralyzed with apprehension. With features set in sick disgust, he clutched the smear on the door-knob, jerked his hand away and groaned.

"Ohh-h-h, Je-s-us!" he said, looking with sick fear at his dripping hand and pawing with his feet at the dry part of the floor. His voice trailed out to the kids clearly, like it does on a clear, cold night. They watched without making a sound.

Mrs. Knowles, precise and prim, stepped to the door.

"What was it, Wellingsford?" she inquired. "Oh—what is that awful smell?"

"Shit!" bellowed Knowles.

Mrs. Knowles didn't understand.

"Don't use such language, Wellingsford," Mrs. Knowles went on. "I said, what is that a-w-f-u-l smell?"

"And, God damn it, woman," howled the old man, "I just told you! It's shit! And, God damn it, it's on me!"

"He-he-he-ha-ha-ha-haw-haw-haw!" screamed Wickie out of the darkness. Old Knowles leaped off the porch and ran toward them like an enraged bull.

"You son of a bitch!" Soapy hollered at Wickie. "Now look what you done! Beat it!"

The kids scattered in all directions. Mark raced over Knowles' back lot, circled the overturned outhouse, and leaped the open vault. Soapy, scrambling after, remembered the vault too late. There was a loud, gummy splash, and Mark looked back to see Soapy, dripping with filth, crawl out of the hole and race on. Mark could not escape the horrible stench. It was everywhere. But he thought of nothing now, save escape.

With no sense of direction the pair raced on through uneven fields of corn stubble, and on out through Kilner's woods. Their breath came in short, winded gasps, and steam poured from tortured lungs. They crashed through thickets and over rock-strewn gullies. At intervals Mark pleaded with Soapy not to touch him. Soapy was covered with slime nearly to his shoulders.

At the creek bank, Soapy, breathing hard, slipped out of his clothing. It was cold, and leaves and twigs about were covered with frost. Steam and fog rolled over the dark water in Yellow Creek, but Soapy plunged right in. He gasped and choked when the water touched his hide.

"Build a fire," he hollered. "It's awful cold."

Mark hastened to build a fire, far up a rocky ravine. Very soon Soapy stood before it, trembling with cold and dripping from head to foot with water. His teeth chattered so that he could not speak, and in the flickering light of the fire, Mark could see that his lips were blue.

"I can't put them clothes back on," he mumbled, after the fire warmed him a bit.

"Did you git it all off'n you?" Mark asked.

"All but from under my fingernails," Soapy said gravely. "Smell'm."

He extended his hands forward. The nails were dark, but his skin was white and clean.

"I don't want to smell'm," Mark said, turning his face away.

Soapy was without clothing, so the night's errand was not ended. Mark gave him his heavy overcoat, and they started back. Soapy shivered under the coat, walking barefooted over the frost-covered leaves.

Feeling guilty, but nevertheless loyal to Soapy, Mark followed the half-naked boy into John Delaney's lumberyard. He kept thinking this was not like stealing chickens for food, and all his training at home surged forth in a conscience-stricken wave. His mind rebelled at Soapy's suggestion they break into Old John's grocery store. They hid for a moment under a pile of lumber. Then Soapy said, "You wait here a minute," and disappeared around the corner of the barn. When he came back he had a long steel crowbar over his shoulder.

"You jist stay hid here," Soapy said, "and listen

and watch everything. If anyone comes, whistle three times and run like hell."

Mark watched with unbelieving eyes as Soapy crept forward, like a young savage. He kept the crowbar thrust before him, and stayed in the shadows. A dim light struggled through the dust-covered windowpane. Soapy slipped the point of the bar under the window and heaved. The window broke its fastening with a thud and slipped upward. Dropping the bar, he leaped, caught the edge of the window, and pulled himself upward. He disappeared inside. Soapy was as agile as a cat.

Now a terrible silence swept over Mark Cullen. It was a silence so ominous that he could hear it. And his heart smote his eardrums until all else was drowned. He listened, alone and afraid, and the impulse to run nearly overpowered him. He wanted to be away from the thing he was doing. Presently he heard footsteps on Delaney Avenue's cinder paths. Nearly choking with fear, he pursed his lips to whistle; hesitated, and listened again. The footsteps went on by, crunched themselves to nothingness in the distance and left behind them only silence again.

Mark's head was wet with sweat, and he no longer felt cold. Panic surged through him, and the needles of conscience stung with almost physical pain. He felt imprisoned, and it seemed hours since Soapy slipped through that window.

"Oh, God," he thought. "Now I'm a burglar—along with everything else."

At first Mark thought it was a man crawling out through the window, for the figure wore a blue overall suit. Then he saw that it was Soapy. Soapy dropped into the shadows and slipped on back to Mark. He handed Mark his overcoat.

"Come on," he whispered. And the two went on out Delaney Avenue. The lights were dark in Cullens' house. Mark climbed on up the trellis and into his room. There was no sound. He undressed silently and climbed into bed.

Mark's conscience tortured him. He could not sleep. Throughout the long night he continued to reassemble events leading up to the burglary of Delaney's grocery store. He visualized himself arrested—spending a long term in the Reform School. His body was tense, and silence sang in his ears. He listened often for the footsteps of Marshal Fogarty coming to arrest him. And finally he watched the red, hateful dawn creep relentlessly over that town.

At breakfast Mark could not eat. He stared straight before him and said nothing. His face was pale, and dark patches lay in half-circles about his eyes. He was eager to be away, and to learn if any of the gang had been arrested. Judy watched him silently as he gulped steaming coffee.

"What's the matter with you, son?" she said finally. "Are you sick? You don't look well."

"I'm awright," Mark gulped.

"He probably needs a physic," Michael observed.

Mark strapped up his books and hastened from the house. Demons prodded his heels, and he ran down Delaney Avenue. When he saw the whole gang in the Delaney Avenue bridge, he felt a little better. Soapy did not wear the blue overall suit, but had on a pair of his old man's pants, cut off at the bottom, and tied about his waist with a rope in a series of ridiculous puckers.

"Don't make no difference what happens," Soapy told all the gang. "Just lie like hell. Don't admit to nothin'. They can't pin nothin' on us. Old Knowles didn't ketch nobody, and he didn't see nobody."

But Mark's soul trembled and the schoolroom swam before his eyes when Marshal Fogarty walked into the room. Marshal Fogarty knew how to use the cop scowl, and he used it now. He did not lift his hat, but scowled from beneath its low brim. No one needed to tell you he was the law. He looked like it. But just the same he hooked his thumbs in his vest, so that his badge showed.

He looked straight at Soapy, and Soapy looked straight at him. There was something in Soapy's eyes that resembled those of a frightened rabbit. But Soapy scowled back, just the same. Fogarty went over to old man Light's desk, and the two held a whispered conversation. Fogarty straightened up and looked at Soapy again, and Light called him.

"Olin," Light said. "Come up here."

Mark was so dizzy with fear that he could scarcely sit upright in his seat. Soapy advanced slowly, looking this way and that, very much like he wanted to escape but could find no means. When he got to the desk, Fogarty grabbed him by the arm and jerked him. Marshal Fogarty acted like he had caught a desperate criminal. Mark waited a long moment, expecting to be called. But the officer led Soapy from the room.

Mark watched out the window, and in just a little while he saw the two of them climbing the Delaney Avenue hill. The marshal still clung to the boy's arm with a heavy paw.

Soapy was gone from Scatterfield a week, and he was lucky he wasn't gone a long time. They kept Soapy in the Juvenile Detention Home in the city. It had bars on the windows, just the same as a jail.

While Michael used the incident to prove to his own son that the paths of evil do not pay, it was nevertheless Michael who saved Soapy from the Reform School. Michael drained the circumstances to the last drop, pouring examples into the ears of Mark Cullen.

"You see what happens to boys whose habits are bad," Michael told Mark. "And you wanted to go out with that gang on Halloween. You see, now, that you were better off in bed."

"Yeah," Mark kept answering him.

The juvenile authorities didn't get anything out of Soapy. They threatened and cajoled, but that dirty kid denied all knowledge of the events of Halloween. He denied it so gracefully and with such insistence that the judge came to doubt it himself. But Soapy's record was against him. J. Wellingsford Knowles urged that the boy be sent away. Michael Cullen risked his job to keep Soapy out of it—and he made an enemy of Knowles by his action.

But with all of Michael's blather, he knew that Soapy had never had a chance. He was sorry for Soapy—but not sorry enough to want Mark to associate with him. With a certain suave grace which was his heritage, Michael overrode the protests of Knowles and influenced the judge to give Soapy a suspended sentence.

"I sentence you to two years in the Reform School," said the judge solemnly. "I'll suspend that sentence on the condition that you obey all laws in the future. Now understand that one false step out of you, and down you go. That's all."

"I never told them nothin'," Soapy told the gang.

"But I can tell ya they hain't goin' ta git me in
that there damned jail agin."

Soapy never forgot the sentence hanging over
his head. He was afraid of it. But the knowledge
did not change his habits. He was a little more
cautious. Nothing more.

"They'll never put me where I can't git out,"
he often said. Long afterward Mark learned that
Soapy meant what he said—that those who caught
up with Soapy had to think fast. Speaking of the
Detention Home to Mark, Soapy crammed a big
chew of tobacco in his jaw.

"Jesus, Mark," he said. "I didn't even git a chaw
all the time I was there."

Thanksgiving Day passed, and the dull days
slipped quietly into weeks. Then winter came
creeping into Scatterfield on stealthy, padded feet.
Swirling, lead-colored clouds began to spit tiny
flecks of snow. Large flakes followed, sweeping
quietly earthward; heaping hills and valleys with
a soft blanket of white silence.

From the Delaney Avenue hill you could see
the brook through a wilderness of falling snow. It
was hedged in now with white, frosty banks. It
wound about aimlessly, pursuing its careless course
toward Yellow Creek. It was fringed a little with
ice, but its dark water looked like a black ribbon
tossed carelessly over a white garment.

Large snowflakes fell thick and fast for a day and a night. Then they thinned, and a blizzard came howling and shrieking out of the northwest. The wind howled like a hungry wolf as it whipped about the corners of rattly buildings. Window-panes clattered. Tar paper ripped loose from houses and flapped a mad tattoo. Muddy ruts in the streets froze and buckled, leaving hard, bone-like ridges and trenches a foot deep.

The wind swept angrily over streets and paths, carrying dense clouds of snow before it, and leaving exposed bare and ulcerlike patches of clay and cinders. Snow banked itself in huge drifts about buildings. Their swordlike tops nearly reached the window ledges of houses.

Scatterfield shivered. Houses creaked and moaned. They trembled in the icy blast but stood, nevertheless, with their faces thrust impudently into the storm. They would survive. They would greet the spring another time—and the warm sun of summer.

The people locked themselves in battered kitchens in such weather as this and drew close to warm cookstoves. They sat at evening staring with dead eyes at red-hot stove tops. They scraped battered chairs across bare floors, drawing closer to the friendly heat.

Old women and kids walked far down the railroad track before dark, gathering coal in buckets and sacks. Their bodies were wrapped in old coats and tattered blankets. Garments too large and too small. Nothing just right. Preserving feeble body heat with old rags.

At school the old jacketed stove devoured scores of buckets of coal. It belched its heat vigorously over part of the room, but in the far corners it was cold. The pipe might be red-hot halfway to the ceiling, but the cold air from out of doors poured through frail siding and around loose windows. You could sit eight feet from the stove with your face burning unpleasantly, and still there would be a chill creeping up your back.

The kids wore just anything that would keep them warm. Some of them wrapped shawls and rags about their necks and ears. Soapy tied his ears in an old flannel cloth, and he wore an overcoat that was meant for a man. It was threadbare and shabby. He looked hunched and formless when he had it on. His father had found it in an alley while gathering junk. The buttons were mostly gone, and Soapy had to hold it about his body. He clutched it through the long sleeves. You couldn't see his hands.

Wickie Winters was about as scantily clad as he had been during warmer weather, but he didn't seem to mind the cold. He had on shoes and stockings, and that was about the only difference. He wore no underwear.

He had a cold—a very bad cold—but Soapy said he always had one in the winter. The frost from his nose streamed down over his wide lips and clear to his chin. He coughed incessantly. Sometimes he coughed so hard that you thought his insides must come up, but he never complained.

Winter weather in Ohio is fickle. It rarely stays that cold more than a week at a time. Sometimes it lasts only a few days. Then it warms a bit and thaws, leaving slush and mud underfoot. After such a thaw Scatterfield looked like an old toothless hag who had been ducked in muddy water.

A few days after the blizzard it grew warmer. But it wasn't warm enough to thaw. Just comfortable. And the long, steep hill along Delaney Avenue was packed down nicely where makeshift sleds had been flying far down into the ravine. The kids thought only of coasting now. During the freeze the high wind had whipped the water in the pond into washboard ice, and it was not possible to skate.

Some of the kids had no sleds, but everyone got to ride. The kids rode belly-gutter—sometimes four deep. Most of the sleds were flimsy home-made crates with wood runners, but the hill was steep and they went fast enough. Harold Knowles had a good sled that his father had bought in a hardware store, but no one wanted to ride with him anyway. The sled had a guider on it, and

Harold always sat upright, placing his feet on the crosspiece. Soapy said it was a hell of a way to ride a sled.

Soapy's sled was made entirely of wood. He had nailed it together himself with lumber and nails filched from Old John Delaney. It was clumsy and hard to pull uphill, but it went down fast enough.

"A hell of a goddam sled," he explained to Mark. "But it's better'n no damn sled at all, hain't it?"

"Yeah," Mark said, thinking that it really *was* better than no sled at all.

Mark's sled was a relic of the old house. He had got it a good many years before moving to Scatterfield. He remembered just when he got it, because it was the year he became confident that there was no Santa Claus.

He had asked Santa to bring him ice skates that year, and he got the sled instead. It was a good sturdy sled with iron runners, and he had caught old Santa up on the deal. He had seen the runners in the village blacksmith shop before Christmas and recognized them immediately when he got the sled. He knew that the blacksmith had made them, and he asked Michael about it. Michael got angry.

"You might as well tell me the truth," he said to his father. "That sled was made in the blacksmith shop for I saw the runners there before Christmas. I know there isn't a Santa Claus."

But Michael never knew when to let up. He was that stubborn he never would admit defeat. He said Mark was a smart alec and that next year he would get nothing. When he finally came down to saying that Santa Claus was the Christmas spirit Mark said that that was about as good as no Santa at all.

The hill was close to the schoolhouse, and all the kids in school coasted there at noon—even the girls. Mark thought it might be a good plan to write Mary Hartman a note about coasting there some night. He never had answered her note. But he felt pretty sure of himself now, since he often caught her looking at him.

A lot of the kids came to the hill at night, too. Mark hadn't been there at night because Michael wouldn't consent to it. He told Mark no one went there at night but a bunch of toughs. Just the same Mark made up his mind to go, even if he had to run away.

He thought he would ask Judy first, though, and maybe she would fix it up. He knew it would be fun at night, because older people came out and built a fire on top of the hill. Soapy went out every night and brought back tales each morning of the sport he had had. He urged Mark to come out.

Finally Mark did write Mary a note. He might

well have asked her outright, but Mark Cullen always liked that romantic touch. He had been thinking about her a good deal—remembering how small and white her hands were. They looked almost like marble, he thought. He really thought it might be nice to hold them. After a long debate with himself he wrote the note.

Dear Mary, he wrote, *I think I am going coasting tonight after supper. Will you be there? Mark Cullen.*

He kept the note in his pocket a long while, fingering it and trying to decide to drop it on her desk. He watched Soapy, but that scalawag didn't seem to be aware of Mark's sinister designs. Once Soapy leaned forward and spit tobacco juice into his inkwell. When Mark looked at Mary she smiled, and he grinned and trembled. Then he flipped the note across his shoulder. He heard it click on her desk.

Dear Mark, came the answer, *Yes, I'll be there, if my father will let me come. Mary.*

Now Mark knew he must go, whatever his father might say.

When he asked Judy she directed him to ask Michael. She wouldn't take the responsibility.

"It's all right with me if your father says you may," she said. "But I don't think he'll want you to go. It'll soon be dark now, so you better get your milking done. Your father is in the barn now."

It wasn't dark yet, but Mark knew it soon would be. He got the milk buckets; the big one and the small one. Michael called the small one the strippings bucket. The strippings came last, and that part of the milk was nearly all cream.

It was murky outside, and the lantern threw its gentle rays in a little, hazy circle on the white snow along the cleanly swept path to the barn.

In Ohio's winter season, darkness comes quickly. In summer it comes trudging slowly over the land like an old man, weary from labor. But in winter it drops suddenly. It swallows the world hungrily.

Mark walked slowly, considering what might be the best approach in bringing up his request to Michael. A gust of wind scooped a cloud of dry, cold snow and hurled it into his face. Then a small whirlwind caught surface snow in a circle dance and hurried it into darkness and dissolution.

The hinges of the barn door squeaked. Then the door banged behind him, and the light from his lantern tossed itself on the straw-covered floor inside.

Michael was moving about in the horse's stall, cleaning it. At intervals he pitched manure out the back door and into a cone-shaped pile. The horse crunched corn, and the cow bawled for hay. The wind whistled sharply around the corner of the barn. Snow swished and rustled gently against the siding.

Mark crawled with the lantern into the hay-mow, and Michael called after him to hurry back with the light. He was working in darkness. Mark pitched hay through the feed holes, and the cow stopped bawling. She tugged and munched at it contentedly.

After Mark came down and started milking, Michael came into the stall.

"How are you getting along in school, Mark?" he asked.

The question, Mark knew, was the prelude to a long discourse on self-discipline and studiousness. Michael had been thinking about his boy, you could tell that. Mark could interpret his every mood.

He had been thinking that circumstances had been treating Mark too kindly. It was Michael's theory that you couldn't achieve unless life was a continual struggle. It was a good thing, according to Michael, for a boy to have a hard time of it—to see the seamy side of life. In this he was vaguely inconsistent. He maintained that most of the kids in Scatterfield were bums and could never amount to much. And the kids in Scatterfield never had known anything but the seamy side of life.

"I'm gettin' along all right, I guess," Mark said.

"I spoke to Mr. Light about you the other day," Michael went on. "He says you do fairly well—

fairly well—except in mathematics. He said you are associated with a class of bad boys, too. And that's got to stop."

Now, hope deserted Mark Cullen. He knew Michael would refuse his request. Mark wouldn't be permitted to go anywhere until his father's resolution had had time to wear off.

"I don't see nothing wrong with the kids," Mark ventured meekly.

And that remark was the trigger which set off the tirade.

"No! Of course, you don't!" Michael howled. "You've taken up all their slang and their dirty ornery habits, too, I suppose. Well, you can just settle yourself—right now! And dig into your mathematics. I'm going to drill you tonight. You're having square root now, aren't you?"

"Yeah," Mark said with feeble indifference.

"Mr. Light isn't such a good mathematics instructor," Michael explained. "But I'll drill it into you tonight until you can work the problems forward and backward."

Mark knew it was useless to ask permission to go out, but he was resolved to do all he could to be right. If that didn't work—and he knew it wouldn't—he was fully determined to go just the same. His mind refused to consider the possible result.

"Well, couldn't you drill me tomorrow night

instead, Pop?" Mark asked hopelessly. "I wanted to go coastin' tonight. Couldn't I do that, Pop— if I get my lessons well first?"

"There it goes!" Michael bellowed.

Then he imitated Mark's voice. He screwed up his features in a gesture meant to imitate a simpleton—meant to represent Mark. In the feeble rays of the lantern he looked very silly. He went on with the mimicking.

"I want to go coastin'. Couldn't I do that, Pop?" he said. "You'll get your lessons and go to bed! That's what you'll do! Running around with all the riffraff in the neighborhood! It's got to stop!

"If I'd have done the things you do when I was a boy, my father would have lammed me within an inch of my life. I worked when I was a boy. If you don't learn to discipline yourself you'll never amount to a hang! But I propose to see that you do.... When I was a boy...."

And so it continued. Mark thrust his head into the cow's side and continued milking silently. He thought his father must never really have been a boy. He couldn't picture him as one. He finished milking and went into the house, leaving the lantern for Michael to bring. Michael would putter about the barn until Judy called him to supper.

After supper Mark pretended to study until Michael lost himself in the evening paper. If the boy were lucky, Michael wouldn't miss him. He would read until the lad got back from the hill. Mark felt that his mother would not betray him. He got his sweater and cap and slipped quietly out the door.

The air was crisp, and the stars above the boy's head blinked with cold detachment. He stood for a moment, drawing on his sweater and adjusting his eartabs. Then he peered cautiously through the window at Michael. With his feet upon the heater Michael was still absorbed in the paper. He read each word and each line slowly. He pulled at the mole on his nose thoughtfully. Mark crept noiselessly around the house, wading in snow ankle deep. Then he got his sled and ran to the hill.

A big bonfire leaped and danced atop the hill, tossing long lances of quivering light toward the valley below. The brook etched itself into banks of snow in the valley like a phantom picture.

It was early, and only a few sleds streaked out of the circle of light and raced down into the shadowy valley. Mary stood by the fire.

"My dad wouldn't have let me come," she explained, "if it hadn't been for you. He said if you were goin' to be here it would be all right, but that I must come home in just a little while."

That made things perfect, Mark reflected, because he must leave soon himself. Besides they could get away before Soapy and the gang came out.

It startled Mark a little when Mary offered to

ride belly-gutter on his back. But when he felt
her body warmly hugged to his own he felt a deep
sense of pleasure. The darkness swam into their
faces, and the wind ripped past their ears.

The valley danced toward them. When the sled
slipped noiselessly to a stop Mark had an impulse
to hold Mary close to him. But the impulse was
drowned in timidity.

They only coasted a few times before Mary said
she would have to go home.

"I won't get to come out again if I don't get
home early," she explained.

So they started out Delaney Avenue, dragging
the sled behind them. Mary clung to the rope, too,
and helped pull it. Mark was relieved when he
successfully navigated the distance past his own
home. He walked a little gingerly there, glancing
apprehensively at the front door.

"Say, Mary," Mark said, after a time. "Did you
mean what you said? I mean about likin' me? In
the note, I mean?"

And Mary Hartman without hesitation or embarrassment answered him at once.

"Sure I meant it," she said. "I do like you."

> *Jesus Christ, what if Soap Dodger Pen-
> dleton could hear you talking that soft stuff,
> Mark Cullen? Jesus!*

"I'm glad you do, because I like you, too," he
gulped.

"I like you better'n any boy in school, I guess," she continued.

"Well, I'm glad of it."

"I don't like that there Soapy Pendleton, though," she said. "He's too darned ornery for his britches. He's like to do *anything*.

"Why I remember one time when he brang four little baby snakes to school and turned 'em loose in the room. They wiggled all over the room and scared everybody to death. They sure was a time until the teacher made him ketch 'em and take 'em out. Soapy got a good licking for it, too. And it was comin' to him."

"Aw, Soapy's a good fellow," Mark said, wishing she wouldn't discuss Soapy. Feeling responsible for taking Soapy's part. "He just likes to play tricks."

"Well, he'd ort to be careful what kind of tricks he's playin'," Mary insisted.

Mark thought he had better change the subject.

"I don't like Scrappy Dolan, I can tell ya that," he said.

"I don't neither," she agreed. "But he hain't no ornrier than most of them there boys in our room."

"He don't like me, neither," said Mark, "and I reckon I'll have to lick him some of these days."

Jesus, Mark Cullen, you said that with a great show of unconcern. It's a good thing she can't see through your sleeve—a good thing she can't see those puny little muscles of yours. Be careful, boy, you're inviting a glance at those spindly legs, too.

"You don't want to go fightin' with Scrappy Dolan. He's bigger'n you," she said. "He's bigger'n you and he might lick you."

"Say," Mark insisted earnestly. "He can't lick me. Just because I ain't big is no sign I can't fight. I got a book that tells all about boxin'. You hit with the muscle in your shoulder. I got good shoulders. You must like Scrappy Dolan— standin' up for him."

Mark, you managed to fool a lot of people throughout your life. But you never fooled yourself. You managed to get people to thinking what you wanted them to think —and you were miserable because those things were not genuine.

"Gee, Mark," she said. "I never meant nothing like that—honest I never. I just thought you were little and I didn't want to see you fight. I never meant nothing by that."

Well, that's pretty soothing. Her regret is genuine. Why don't you feel just right about it? Slam into it and beat your skinny chest. Maybe you can someday believe that stuff yourself.

"You believe me, don't you, Mark? I just don't want you to be hurt."

*There you are, standing right in front of
her house. You can see that she is embarrassed and that she really likes you. You
like that feeling. You're king, now. But
listen, that's just the mother instinct. She's
sorry for you, just as all women were
throughout your life. You wanted to be a
big he-man and that's the best you could
awaken in them. Don't you feel a little ridiculous about it all?*

"You'n kiss me good-by if you want to, Mark,"
she said very simply.

*You felt her warm body close to your
own. What made you tremble when you
held your lips to hers? Your loins surged
and you were ashamed. You did not understand the impulses of the body. Only for
a moment, and a lance of light leaps across
the white, white snow. The door is closed
and she is gone. The door is closed.*

Mark Cullen walked slowly home, his head swimming. There were mighty thoughts racing through
the boy's mind that night as he walked under the
high, cold dome of the sky. And there were clouds
in that sky rolling and changing from one shape
to the other—just as all things change.

Huge snowdrifts that lay along that street in
Scatterfield so long ago were like lovely white
women abed—sleeping in delicious silence. The
wind rolled restlessly down Delaney Avenue, carry-

ing clouds of snow before it—hurling them into Mark's face. Ah, that, too, was a grand gesture.

All that fine imagery was jolted out of his mind soon enough. When he reached home he saw Michael standing just inside the yard with a buggy whip in his hand.

Mark Cullen wanted to reach out an imploring hand to Michael and beg him not to destroy the thing in his mind. But it was useless. Mark knew this. Mark walked slowly toward his father— feeling weak—walking slowly toward Michael Cullen—saying nothing. As Mark opened the gate Michael clasped his shoulder with a heavy hand. All feeling was gone, now.

"I thought I told you ... (whack! whack! whack!) disobey me ... (whack! whack! whack!) running around ... (whack! whack! whack!) roughnecks in the ... (whack! whack! whack!)"

Michael Cullen thought he was doing right. Michael Cullen never did anything in his life which he could not justify. He was breathing hard now. Mark, you pulled your shoulders far up so that your head was buried deep, like that of a turtle. You said nothing. Not a word said Mark Cullen— not a sob.

Michael ceased his labor a moment.

"Are you going to disobey me again?" he inquired. And his breath came in labored gasps. It was hard work for Michael Cullen to beat his boy that way.

Mark did not answer. He pulled his head further into his bony shoulders.

"Are you? Are you?" (Whack! whack! whack!)

And never a word said Mark.

"Now you get in there and get to bed!" bellowed Michael.

Mark left his sled in the front yard and walked slowly in the door. He walked on upstairs to his room. Judy watched, and in her eyes was that old haunted look. Fear centered in the eyes of Judy Cullen, and she said no word. She only watched silently, but she did not follow.

Mark locked his door and lit his lamp. Then he sat for a long time staring with dull eyes into the corner of the room. A mottled little ball of dust lay there, and with his eyes he traced and re-traced its weblike core.

He walked to the window and looked out into the moonlit night. His sled lay beside the walk where he had left it. The tracks left by the runners led to the gate. Beside the sled were two deeply imbedded footprints—Mark's own. There he had stood with his head drawn tortoise-like into his shoulders and taken his lashing. About the two small footprints were many larger ones. Michael had changed his position numerous times during the ordeal.

Mark turned away and sat on his bed. He took off his shoes and stockings. He gazed long and silently at his legs striped with large, red welts. They were skinny legs—thin and pinched little legs—and Mark remembered how horribly ashamed of them he always was. Now they were covered with large, red welts and were uglier than ever.

He ran the palm of his hand over their lumpy surface. The skin was broken in several places. He watched his hand as though it were not a part of his body. It, too, was thin, and the bones traced themselves clearly through it.

How horribly skinny he was! His chin quivered, and he began to sob violently. He lay back on his bed and clenched his pillow. His frail body shook as with an involuntary spasm.

In another moment he heard Judy at his door, trying the knob. But the door was locked.

"I've got some popcorn here, Mark," she called through the panel. "Do you want some popcorn?"

Mark controlled his sobbing for only a moment. "No, Ma'm," he said.

"Do you want me to bring you anything, Mark?" she asked anxiously. "Is there anything you want?"

"No, Ma'm."

He then heard her retracing her steps—heard her talking to Michael downstairs. But he didn't try to understand what they were saying.

Now Mark felt a sense of utter dejection—of

irrevocable defeat. He called to mind a great many things Michael had done in the past. Things done thoughtlessly—things Mark never forgot throughout all his life.

He remembered the calf Michael had once given him at the old house with the promise that he should do what he would with it if he took good care of the animal. He made a pet of the calf; fed and watered it carefully. Then Michael sold it and kept the money.

And there were times without number when Michael had promised to take the boy somewhere and never got around to it.

"I'm going to take you fishing Saturday," he would say.

And throughout the week Mark would look eagerly forward to the trip. But when Saturday finally came there was always something else more important, and the trip always was postponed.

Gradually Mark got to disregarding such promises.

"Do you want to go with me Saturday to. . . ?"

And to that question Mark got to answering, "Yeah," and promptly forgetting about it.

But Mark would have liked it. He would have liked being alone with his father and talking about things. It would have been like knowing him better. But when Mark Cullen grew older it was too late. And Michael Cullen never knew what his boy might have been to him.

After a long time when Mark's sobs had dwindled into long-drawn involuntary sighs, Michael came up the stairs and called through the door panel.

"I'm sorry I had to tan you, Mark," he said. "But you must learn to mind. It hurt me worse than it did you. You'll know what I mean sometime. I don't like to tan you."

Mark didn't believe what he said. Michael never whipped him except when he was angry. The boy considered his remark an untruth.

The whipping had done something to his mind. It always did. It would be a long time before Mark Cullen would be having any dream pictures again. He would be going around with a sense of frustration and defeat and wouldn't enjoy much of anything. But he would finally get over it.

Now, he heard Michael in his own bedroom launching into a long and uninterrupted sermon— explaining why to Judy. Mark covered his ears with a pillow so that he couldn't hear the voice. After a long, long time he fell asleep.

It was a pretty dull Christmas that year in Scatterfield. It was over now, and Mark Cullen was not sorry. He was sorry, though, that the weather had turned out so badly. Three days of Christmas vacation were already gone and he had only been out of the house to do the chores.

Leaden clouds had covered the sky all that time, and rain and sleet alternately had poured over the hovels in town, lashing them with the fury of a sadistic giant. There had been little to do save stay in the house. Mark hadn't seen Soap Dodger Pendleton or any of the Scatterfield gang since the Christmas Eve party at the schoolhouse.

That party hadn't amounted to much, and Mark had to laugh when he thought of it. Michael had thought it a solemn duty to make a speech. The room was crowded with ragged kids and their parents. The older people hadn't bothered to clean up much, and most of the men were still dressed in their working clothes. They had washed their faces, but shop grease still clung about their eyes, which made them appear to be staring.

Michael had screwed up his face into a mass of earnest-looking wrinkles, pulled energetically at the mole on his nose, and talked for nearly an hour.

He said that the noblest life of all was that of labor and quoted Longfellow's "The Village Blacksmith" to prove it. He covered all the rules of right living and brought in a little autobiography to illustrate how right living always triumphs and perseverance will usually bring you to the top— or at least nearly there.

Then he started talking about the Scatterfield

kids. He said that there were no better children anywhere on the face of the earth.

Michael grew pretty mellow at the last and said that God often spoke in the voices of children; that they were free from guile and that grown persons might well learn a serious lesson from them. Everyone had listened pretty patiently. But they hadn't heard the speech so often as Mark had heard it.

After Michael finished the speech, Old John Delaney had come into the room with a pack on his back. He was dressed like Santa Claus. That made everyone laugh. There wasn't a person in the room who hadn't been cheated by the old man at some time or other. It was a big joke to think of him as Santa.

But he didn't fool anybody—not even the little kids. They all knew him. You couldn't mistake those red cheeks with purple veins running through them—or the bulbous nose. His whisky breath smelled natural, too.

There had been a present for each kid—a box of hard candy and something else, nicely wrapped in tissue paper. Old John handed them out as though he had been accustomed to giving things away every day.

When Mark tore open his package he found a top, and he didn't care anything about tops. He showed it to Soapy, and Soapy laughed. Then Soapy tore open his own package.

"Jesus Christ!" Soapy said.

It was a rag doll with big, blue eyes and long, black lashes painted about them like spider legs. Only its face was painted, and the rest of its little naked body didn't have a mark on it.

"I wonder what the hell it is," Soapy had said, "a boy or a girl. You can't tell by lookin' at it. I reckon it must be a morphodite."

He asked Mark if he knew what a morphodite was and Mark said yes. Then he took its soft little arms and wriggled them about and made the doll thumb its nose at Mark.

"A awful purty little critter to be a-doin' sech ornery things, hain't it?" he snickered.

Soapy and Mark had sat down together in one of the seats, and Soapy began to fasten all the appendages on the doll that belonged to it. Part of them he drew with ink and part of them he fashioned with tablet paper, pinning them on.

While he was at work with it, Mark kept looking around at Mary Hartman. He hoped that he could get away and walk home with Mary, but he didn't get to. He couldn't leave Soapy. Soapy was his best friend. He would have made fun of Mark anyway —walking home with a girl.

Soapy had finally got the doll to look more natural, and the two kids sat there until they finished all their candy. The doll he placed on the desk where everyone could see it. It stared at the people with big, innocent-looking eyes, but it seemed a little shameless with all those things fastened to it.

After the two boys got through with the candy, Soapy crammed his mouth full of scrap tobacco on top of the sweet taste.

On the way home Soapy had tied the doll's legs around its neck and tossed it into the brook. Mark tossed his top in after it. He didn't want a top. But he hadn't got to walk home with Mary. Soapy had stayed with him to his front gate.

All that had happened three days ago, and nothing much had happened since—except Christmas, but Mark didn't get much that year. He got a pair of ice skates and a sweater and a set of the works of Edgar Allan Poe. He couldn't use the skates in such weather as this, and he would have got the sweater anyway. The books were nice, though, and he was glad to have them. They helped while away the tedious time.

Because it was Christmas week Michael had left Mark to himself and hadn't lectured him once. Mark reflected that his father usually eased up on discipline when there wasn't anything to do anyway.

The boy had been reading Poe's weird stories and some of his poems. In the midafternoon he had stopped reading awhile to look out the window and to think about what he had read. He was in his own room, where the coal stove was so hot that he had to raise the window. It had warmed quite a bit out of doors, and the snow was melting.

Scatterfield was wearing a pretty bedraggled garment that day. The wet snow was mottled with a thick coating of black soot, and a great many muddy pools of water stood about in hollow depressions. It was so very still outside that Mark could hear water dripping, like mournful tears, from the corners of old Mrs. Hessenauer's house across the street. It was washing a deep trench in the dirty snow about the building. Yellow clay showed up in spots throughout the yard; ulcerous spots, like human flesh in decay.

Old Mrs. Hessenauer was in her woodshed back of her house, chopping kindling. She held a hand axe, and Mark could hear it click-clack against the wood. He could only see part of her figure silhouetted against the window beyond. He knew that her old hands were swollen with rheumatism and that her work was painful.

Last autumn she had been so crippled with rheumatism that she had had to crawl out to dig her potatoes. There was a lumpy, uneven place in the yard where the garden had been and where now some of the half-decayed vegetation stuck through the dirty snow like whiskers in dead flesh.

After a little while Mark heard snow break loose

from a slanting roof on up the street. He looked.
It groaned and slipped to the ground with a loud
ker-r-rump! It banked itself in the dirty slush
beneath.

The whole town looked bleak and deserted of
everything pleasant, but Mark wasn't really seeing
it now. His eyes wandered about, fastening on this
and that, but the picture didn't stamp itself into
his mind.

The lines of a poem he had been reading kept
tumbling about in his brain and transforming
everything he saw. He had been reading Poe's
"Annabel Lee" and thinking about Mary Hartman. He felt a little melancholy, and as each word
of the poem drifted into his mind he fondled it,
sounded out the rhythm, and released it.

> It was many and many a year ago,
>   In a kingdom by the sea
> That a maiden there lived whom you may know
>   By the name of Annabel Lee;
> And this maiden she lived for no other thought
>   Than to love and be loved by me.

Mark thought he never had read anything so
pretty. It certainly made him think of Mary, and
he wished that her name would rhyme with the
rest of the poem so that he could substitute it for
Annabel Lee.

His eyes were tired from reading. He stood at
the window and gouged and rubbed them with his

clenched fist. Michael and Judy were talking down-stairs, but he didn't try to hear them. Their voices droned in his ears from very far away. They seemed far away.

He began to conjure up a picture of the kingdom by the sea. He had never seen a kingdom, but he began to build one according to his notion of what it ought to be. It was easier to think of it as being right there in Scatterfield. Probably the yellow-bellied water pond back of the schoolhouse was the sea. No, it wasn't the sea, but that was the place. That's where the sea lay, but it was very much larger than the water pond and different in every way. The water was blue, not yellow, and far, far out the sparkling waves leaped and touched the sky. They rolled in from 'way out there and lashed the shore. They boomed and roared against crags and rocks.

Mark sat down, thinking hard. The fire in his stove was dying down, and the air, chill and damp, crept through the window. A wagon creaked and rattled in front of the house, and a teamster shouted.

"Gee up there, damn you!" he yelled.

He heard a blacksnake whip crack and looked out the window into Delaney Avenue. It was a load of lumber from Old John Delaney's lumber yard going up to Clara Street where the old man was building a new house. The horses were skinny, with sides that heaved like bellows. Sweat poured from their flanks in little rivulets, and their feet sank deep into the mud. The harness chains jangled and creaked, and the wheels of the wagon sank nearly to the hubs. No snow in Delaney Avenue now. It had been whipped away, leaving long, muddy ruts and holes. The teamster wore rubber boots and walked beside the wagon, sparing the laboring team the weight of his body.

A wagon going up to Clara Street. That's where Mary lived.

> And this is the reason that, long ago,
> In this kingdom by the sea,
> A wind blew out of a cloud, chilling
> My beautiful Annabel Lee;
> So that her high-born kinsmen came
> And bore her away from me,
> To shut her up in a sepulchre
> In this kingdom by the sea.

He tried to see Mary's house, but another obscured it. He could see the outhouse in the rear, though. A narrow, little outhouse, leaning far to one side.

He didn't want to see it, and he had to turn away and hurry to force the picture out of his mind. He knew that it could very easily shatter the kingdom which he was so carefully building. He didn't permit his mind to conjure any details about that outhouse. He turned away from the window and shut it out of his mind. He just quit thinking about it.

He thought, now, that he would go to the barn and crawl into the haymow. He could be alone there, with no noises jarring on his ears. He went downstairs and put on his new sweater. Michael sat before the stove in an armchair. He had just picked up the paper, and he glanced at Mark and pulled thoughtfully at the mole on his nose. He put on his half-moon spectacles and said nothing. He didn't even ask where the boy was going. It was Christmas week, Mark reflected; that was the reason. Mark went through the kitchen and out the back door. Judy was on her hands and knees, scrubbing the kitchen floor.

"Put on your rubbers, son, if you're going out," she called out after the boy.

His rubbers were on the back porch, but he didn't bother to put them on. She didn't come to see.

He walked through the slush to the barn. The snow in the backyard was pockmarked with soot and melted places. A pile of ashes lay heaped at one corner of the barn with water dripping into it from the cornice above. The air was heavy with grey mist, and it was very quiet. Mark couldn't hear anything except water dripping monotonously into the half-melted snow.

The horse neighed anxiously when he opened the barn door. The cow fixed her big, brown eyes on him inquiringly. Then she turned about with unconcern and resumed munching the hay in her manger.

Mark crawled to the loft and lay down in the soft hay. Rats scurried about far beneath. Their tails thumped the floor, and they squealed loudly. Then everything was still.

> But our love it was stronger by far than the love
>   Of those who were older than we—
>   Of many far wiser than we—
> And neither the angels in heaven above,
>   Nor the demons down under the sea,
> Can ever dissever my soul from the soul
>   Of the beautiful Annabel Lee. . . .

Words invaded his mind and churned about restlessly. Words transforming themselves into pictures. Mary Hartman with her taffy-colored hair and blue eyes. It certainly was a beautiful poem, Mark thought.

He hadn't ever said that he *loved* Mary. The word sounded pretty silly, anyway, but he certainly *liked* Mary very much. Just the same, the word didn't sound silly in that poem, and he repeated the lines over and over again, thinking of her. Then he contrived to place a castle on Clara Street where Mary lived; a high-turreted castle whose spires reached far into the blue sky.

Mary's face kept swimming before his eyes, and in a little while he got to thinking it would be nice to really see her. He hadn't thought that very long before it became a near necessity.

He couldn't think of an excuse except that he might go up and ask her to go coasting with him. He thought maybe the hill had melted too much for coasting, but they could go out and try it. It wouldn't be long before dark, and he'd have to hurry. He crawled down out of the mow, got his sled, and started up Delaney Avenue toward Clara Street.

The cinder path was covered with slush, and it wasn't long before his feet were wet. There were big, black spots on the cinder path where the snow had melted entirely away, leaving little pools of water. The ground had thawed beneath the path, and when he walked over it the cinders weaved up and down in their soft bed. The runners of his sled struck the bare places with a rasping noise that made chills race up and down his spine.

When he got to Mary's house he walked past without even looking in. Up the street a way he turned about and walked back, dragging his sled behind him. He looked in this time, but didn't see anyone. The house looked dark and gloomy. He started to walk again and then turned back.

"Mary," he called with such timidity that you couldn't have heard him ten feet away.

Everything was quiet, and he stood twisting about on one foot, gathering courage really to call her.

"Mary!" he finally yelled. "Aw, Mary!"

She came out this time, and Mark asked her to go coasting with him. She raised no objection at all. She said nothing about the snow being almost gone. She just said "Sure," and went in and put on her sweater and came along. She took hold of the rope on Mark's sled and helped pull it.

"What did you get for Christmas?" Mark asked her.

"I jist got some dresses and things," she answered vaguely, "and we had a awful good chicken dinner. I eat so much I like to bust. What did you get?"

"Oh, I didn't get much," Mark said. "I just got a sweater and some skates and some books. There was some awful pretty po'ms in one of the books. One of 'em made me think about you."

"Did it, honest? What was it about?"

"I'll tell it to you," he said. And he recited the whole poem, elated at using the word *love* and feeling natural about it because it was really someone else using it. Someone else using it for Mark.

"Hain't it pretty?" he asked when he had finished his recitation.

"Did it really make you think of me?" she asked.

"Yeah. It's pretty po'm, hain't it?"

"Uh-huh, it's awful pretty. I like it all right. But I don't like most po'ms. I can't get no sense out of 'em."

The hill along Delaney Avenue where the kids

had coasted last week didn't look inviting now. Long marks left by sled runners cut through it clear to the valley, and they were dark-looking now, and overrun with little streams of water rushing toward the brook below. There was scarcely a patch of dry snow left. The hillside was mostly covered with grey, soggy slush.

The dead and blackened embers of a bonfire lay scattered about in a wide circle. Within the circle the snow was completely gone, and save for tufts of dead grass and weeds it looked naked.

Mark had been thinking of the hill as a high mountain, rearing its shoulders far above the sea.

> It was many and many a year ago
> In a kingdom by the sea. . . .

Overhead grey clouds rolled and tumbled. Darkness would soon be there, and if Mark and Mary were going to coast they must hurry. The brook would soon be out of banks. The snow would soon be gone.

The water pond back of the schoolhouse—a turbulent sea, dashing against an impenetrable wall of rock. . . . Words churning about in Mark's mind, painting a curious picture of the kingdom by the sea.

A narrow strip over one side of the hill looked like it might be solid enough to hold the sled runners, and Mark said they would try it.

They slipped away and started flying down the hill, the wind screaming in their ears. The sled churned the slush and tossed a trail of spew behind them. Mary clung to Mark and giggled.

About half way down the runners broke through the surface snow and caught in the soggy clay beneath, bringing the sled to a sudden stop. They both went head over heels, rolling and tumbling in the water.

When Mark scrambled to his feet he caught a glimpse of something that disturbed him. Mary's dress had blown up, and he caught a fleeting glimpse of her drawers, bulging and bagging at the tops of her stockings. The drawers looked a little dirty, and on one leg, just above the stocking top, there was a large spot which resembled grease.

Mark began to struggle, now, to force the picture of them out of his mind. Clean gingham apron and dirty drawers beneath. It was pretty damaging to the kingdom by the sea. He struggled hard, forcing it little by little out of his brain.

> That the wind came out of a cloud by night
> Chilling and killing my Annabel Lee....

"There hain't no use tryin' ta coast," he said finally. "It's goin' ta git dark pretty soon anyhow, an' I got ta git home before dark. I guess we might as well git goin'."

"All right," Mary agreed. "That sure was some spill we took, wasn't it?"

She squinted up her nose and grinned.

Scatterfield looked pretty dreary to Mark as they walked up Delaney Avenue.

Dirty drawers bulging where they had been crammed into black stockings.

Oil lamps began to appear in kitchen windows, throwing their dull, sickly light through the mist. Mark's clothing was drenched, and the damp air clutched at him with a clammy hand. He shivered and continued to build at his kingdom. But it was difficult to keep out the other picture. It had taken root in a fleeting glimpse and was striving to grow.

They had walked silently for a time and were nearly to Mary's house when she stopped suddenly and grinned. Then she squinted up her nose in a grimace of discomfort and reached for her backside and pulled at her dress; pulled *through* her dress and tugged at something.

"When I fell off'n that there sled I sure set in the water," she said. "Gosh, but my pants is wet and sticky."

She stepped gingerly about and tugged at the sticky seat.

Now the ruin was complete. Scatterfield wasn't a kingdom, and you couldn't make one out of it.

Wet drawers clinging tenaciously to two little red buttocks—goose flesh and wet drawers. He could see the whole thing as clearly as though she had shown him. He felt a little sick.

Scatterfield was just a town of rattly shacks and muddy streets. A barren, lonely town; indecent and naked, sprawled over hills of yellow clay. Its streets were like horrible wounds; its people like insect lice on the body of a ragged beggar. He felt resentful and mean.

Mary was all unaware of what Mark had been thinking, and they stood for a moment before her house. She twisted her body coyly about and smiled amiably, but Mark was far away from such charms —far away, drowned in desolation and despair. He heard her voice. She was talking to him, and he at last drew up his mind to attention.

"It's dark enough so'st you can kiss me good-by," she was saying.

Everything was turned about in his mind, and he wasn't thinking coherently. He saw the outhouse in the backyard, tipped precariously to one side. It was pretty close to the back door, and the yard looked muddy and bedraggled.

Cold wet buttocks—little ones, with drawers sticking to them, and a battered old outhouse too close to the back door. It was gloomy and dark.

It was many and many a year ago. . . .

"I don't wanna kiss ya," he said.

"Why?" she asked, looking puzzled. "Whut'd I do?"

Mark didn't know what she had done, but he felt a little weary and remembered that his eyes were tired from reading.

"You just didn't do nothing," he said at last. "I just don't like you no more."

"Oh!" she said. Then she turned quickly away from him and ran into the house.

He stood for a long time, staring dumbly about him. The faded light from an old oil lamp came through the front window, and he looked inside. Mary's father sat before the coal heater, nodding contentedly. His hands were folded over his heavy paunch, and his teeth ground monotonously on a big chew of tobacco.

> So that her high-born kinsmen came
> And bore her away from me. . . .

The old man leaned forward and opened the stove door. The fire flushed his face crimson, and shadows leaped merrily about his bald head. He spat tobacco juice into the fire and wiped his mouth with the back of a grimy hand. He closed the door and leaned back contentedly again. He needed shaving.

Mark began now to feel a little ashamed of himself for having talked that way to Mary. She had looked puzzled and hurt. It wasn't her fault, but Mark couldn't help it either. He just felt that way, and that's all there was to it.

He looked again at the house. It certainly wasn't a high-turreted castle. It was just a little shack; not much more, and part of the clapboard siding was loose and it needed painting. The shingles on the roof were old and worn. Some of them were missing.

Just the same Mark felt contemptible about the way he felt toward Mary. He was just a baby to feel that way. He turned about and started out through the slush. His feet were soaked through, and he felt cold. His sled rasped over naked spots in the cinder path, and cold water seeped through his shoes. He wished now that he might feel natural about things, like Soap Dodger Pendleton. He guessed he had been reading too much the last several days.

"Aw, hell!" he said aloud.

He guessed he would hunt Soapy up tomorrow and get him to go down to Yellow Creek with him. Maybe Soapy could take his old man's rifle. They could knock over a couple of squirrels down at Yellow Creek tomorrow, maybe. Mark had been reading too damn much lately—that's what was the matter with him.

Spring comes late in Ohio some years. Winter

drags along until June. It did that year. There had been cold rains and even snow all through May in Scatterfield. Now in the middle of June there were three or four really hot days. The people crawled out from the warmth of their battered kitchens like a swarm of lazy flies. The streets were still thick with yellow oozy mud, but patches of green showed up here and there on the bleak hills. It was a portent of nice weather.

School had been out for two weeks, and most of that time the Scatterfield gang found nothing better to do than loaf around in Old John Delaney's lumberyard. Old John didn't allow them in there, but the place was like a jungle, and he couldn't find them. They even knew where he hid his whisky bottle. They watched every step he took.

Soap Dodger Pendleton played a good many mean tricks on Old John, but he deserved most of them. Old John was suave, and at first you thought he was fine, but when you really got to know him it was a different story. And Soapy played a good many practical jokes on him. Soapy never laughed about them, though. He just watched the effects of the joke and looked satisfied. Once he got the old man's whisky bottle and poured half of it out. Then he filled it up with something else. That *was* a mean trick. But Soapy crawled back under a pile of lumber and waited for John to come for a drink. All the gang sat on their haunches and peered out through the rain, waiting for John to come out.

It wasn't long. He came wading out through the thick mud. His old bowlegs were in a hurry. He reached up to the place where he kept the bottle, peering around all the time to see if anyone could see him from the back door of his dirty old grocery store.

Mark looked at Soapy. He was watching with the keenest of interest. Soapy even forgot to chew on the great cud of tobacco in his cheek. Delaney took a long pull at the bottle, and then he nearly strangled. He coughed and wheezed, and his face got so red that for a while the little red and blue veins in his cheeks disappeared.

Mark Cullen didn't know whether the old man knew what was in the bottle, but he threw it as far as he could see it. Then he turned around and splashed off through the mud. He kept coughing and spitting like he had had something dirty in his mouth. Soapy watched him, and when he was gone, he shifted his chew into the other cheek. He squirted a great stream of tobacco juice and ran a dirty paw around under his chin. He took a deep breath and said, "Come on, fellers, let's git outa here." He acted just like a person who had set out to do a fine piece of work and accomplished it. Soapy was mean in some ways, but he never smiled about his meanness. Old John was meaner than Soapy, and he tried to hide it with gentility.

But now with the bright June sun wiping away the grey clouds, there was plenty to do, and Old John got a rest. The gang didn't have to wait any longer. Soapy said he hadn't had a bath all winter, and none of the kids doubted his word. They went swimming that very day up at Yellow Banks, a mile above Scatterfield. The water was thirty feet deep there, and swift, too. The creek was hedged in by high clay banks. When the water was low the banks were fifteen feet high and straight down. The kids dived in and swam with the current clear to the floodgate.

None of the boys could dive like Soapy. They usually lit belly-gutter with a loud, painful splash. But there was hardly a splash when he lit. He wasn't a fancy diver—he just hit the water easily, like a frog, and it leaped about a foot where his body disappeared.

Soapy always dived under the floodgate, too. He was lucky not to catch himself on the old logs lying against the gate below the surface. That would have been the end of him, because the strong current would have held him there. Soapy was a good swimmer.

The kids didn't stay in long that day. The water was as cold as ice. It hadn't had time to warm up. They were glad to get their clothes on and get out from beneath the shade of the towering willows along Yellow Banks. The sun was warm.

Nutsie Doane said that his father had been out of work a long while and that the family hadn't been eating much. He said he really felt a little hungry after that swim. The corn in the bottoms along Yellow Creek wasn't up but an inch above ground. It was only up in spots, too, because the frost had nipped a good bit of it.

The gang knew that Old Farmer Castell had some fine Leghorn chickens, and they borrowed one. They were not very lucky that day. They got an old hen. But the hen was better than nothing, so they wrung her neck and ripped out as many feathers as possible.

They built a good fire and packed the hen in mud and roasted her. They let her cook a long time, and when they raked her out of the fire the baked clay dropped off and left the tender meat.

When they ate down to where the entrails were, they found an egg fully developed and cooked to a turn. Nutsie Doane ate the egg. Nutsie always looked hungry whether he was or not. He had big, famished-looking, brown eyes, and his olive skin clung tightly to the bones in his cheeks. He was really hungry that day, though. He ate like a hungry boy.

When they got through with the chicken they sat around and talked. Soapy Pendleton pulled

out a package of scrap tobacco. There was a man-
sized chew in it—enough for two chews—but
Soapy crammed all of it into his cheek. He looked
cleaner now, but the chew made him look more
natural. Cockie Werner had three cigarettes, and
he broke each of them in two. All the gang smoked
now except Soapy. He chewed. The rest of the
kids had all had a try at chewing, but without success. Mark would never forget his try. But the
boys all envied Soapy secretly.

The sun was still high in the sky when they started
back. They came back through Kilner's Woods.
They rarely went back the other way, although it
was shorter, because they had to pass the Hunt
shack. The Hunt boys always shot at them with a
rifle. Mark Cullen always thought the Hunts a
queer lot. They wouldn't speak to anyone, and
they shot at everyone who came past their shack.
They shot at people when they weren't even on
their property. Mark Cullen, for one, didn't like
to listen to bullets whistling over his head. The
gang almost never went back that way.

Kilner's Woods wasn't really a woods; just a
grove of trees—mostly beech—but people in Scatterfield called it a woods.

Cockie had a long whang leather slingshot, and
he kept throwing at birds with it. He used stones
about the size of goose eggs. Mark had a shinny
club that he had cut from a hickory sapling along

in the fall. He had carved it handsomely and had seasoned it in the kitchen behind the stove.

Wickie Winters didn't have anything at all. He never did have. But the gang always remembered that Wickie didn't even know as much as he might have known. He just walked along with the rest of the kids, looking vaguely at things and chattering like a monkey. He laughed loudly at things that weren't funny at all. The top of his head was wide, and his forehead was low. His ears were set 'way up on top of his head, and his little eyes danced wildly about trying to see everything at once.

Soapy chewed his tobacco and spat against the trunks of trees.

Before Charlie Heston's shanty there was a long slope. It led clear up to the top of the hill, and the shanty leaned and tipped ominously at the very crest. You could see the whole town from the shanty door. It wasn't really in Scatterfield, but you could see the whole town from it.

When the kids came up the slope, Charlie was sitting in the doorway making figures on a pad. And the kids knew that he was devising a way of improving his interest table. Charlie was a wizard at figures, and he hoped to make a good deal of money from that table. All the problems you could work on it, he could work in his head, giving you the answer right off. But he said it was a handy thing, and that most people needed it. He said further that it was the best table in existence.

Back of him in the doorway sat his little wasp-like wife in a rocking chair. She rocked and gazed wearily over the yellow valley below, and to the graveyard far on the other hill. Her face was white and expressionless. She looked like a marble statue.

When Charlie saw that Scatterfield gang he got a bucket and pumped some water for them. He always did that, and many times it tasted good to the kids. The old woman didn't speak to them at all. She never did. She just sat there rocking silently in the doorway. But Old Charlie talked incessantly. He said there would be nice weather now, and that the frost had killed his sweet corn, and that he would have to replant the whole damned thing. The kids answered him by saying, "Yeah, yeah, yeah."

They liked the old man. He was always good to them. He was good to everyone. Most people said he would have amounted to a great deal if it hadn't been for his drinking. They said that many years ago he had taught a class in astronomy in an Eastern university, but he didn't try to teach anyone anything in Scatterfield. J. Wellingsford Knowles said that all such talk was just a pretty way of making excuses for a worthless old man, but the kids didn't care what he said. They liked the old fellow. He was always good to them.

They stood there and drank the water. They drank it just because he got it. Soapy held his chew in his hand while he drank, because he didn't have another. Mark drank first and walked to the edge of the hill. He could see the whole town stretched out there in the bright sunlight like a dirty human body. . . . It was like a beggar sleeping in a palace for Scatterfield to stretch itself out there under that bright June sun. In such a light as this the yellow clay reflected itself in the faces of the people. They looked bilious.

In the south part of town Mark could see John Delaney's apple orchard. The part that was alive, which wasn't much, had sickly blossoms on it. He could barely see the little patches of white mixed in with the green. The great splotches of brown that showed up here and there were dead trees. Old John always said the blossoms were fragrant, but Mark thought they were really too small to be anything.

The sunlight accentuated the poverty-ridden hovels and shacks. The streets were still muddy, and the yellow brook still rushed madly through the valley below them. In a few days the brook would be dried up, and the mud in the streets would turn to yellow dust. The people in Scatterfield would breathe it all summer.

Old Charlie came up and stood beside Mark. He looked at the town before them for a long while.

Mark, watching him sideways, saw that he looked haggard, and it seemed that his eyes were sad. After a while he turned to Mark and smiled in his peculiar way.

"The city of the seven hills," he said.

"Yeah," answered Mark, thinking that there were more than seven of them.

Then Cockie came up there with them and shot a big stone far down the valley with his sling. The muddy water splashed 'way down there where it lit in the brook. Then everybody said good-by to Charlie and went down that way. Mark looked back when he got to the bottom of the hill, and the old man was still standing there. His pale-faced wife was still rocking in the doorway.

The gang cut across to Perry Street. Soapy said he wanted to stop at Limpy Peters' drugstore for a package of scrap tobacco. Mark wondered where he got the nickel, but didn't ask him.

Limpy's drugstore was one story high and had a slanting roof. The building was painted the dull red you see on old barns in Ohio. It had a window on each side of the door. In each window hung a sign reading: A. C. PETERS, DRUGS & SODAS. Limpy was careless about the way the store looked inside, but he didn't have to be any other way. Everybody was careless in Scatterfield. The whole gang went in. The inside smelled cool, and the oiled floor felt good to Mark's bare feet.

Limpy Peters' left leg was considerably shorter than his right one, and it was bent at the knee. When he walked he placed his left hand on the crippled knee and seemed to push the withered foot to the ground. At the same time his hindside bobbed up in the air. When Mark saw him walking around he always thought of a railroad handcar.

"Give me a package of scrap tobacco for my pa," Soapy said.

"Are you sure it's for your pa, Soapy?" he asked.

"If I say so that lets you out, don't it, Limpy?" Soapy said. "Anyway, I don't chew."

"What's that you got tucked in your jaw?" Limpy asked.

"That ain't nothin', Limpy. That's just the way my jaw is made."

"Well, I just wondered."

After the gang came out Mark spoke to Soapy.

"Soapy," he said, "did you ever notice that Limpy smells just like his drugstore?"

"Sure," he answered. "Every guy smells like his work."

Wickie danced and jiggled around. He hollered, "He-he-ha-ha-ha-haw-haw-haw!"

"Shut up, you goddam fool!" howled Cockie.

"How do you mean, Soapy?" Mark asked.

"Well, my old man deals in junk and he smells like old rags," Soapy explained. "Limpy smells like his drugstore. Doctor Clarke smells like medicine."

Mister Holt is a undertaker and he smells sweet,
like a funeral. Them guys that works in the fac-
tories in the city smells like smoke and grease.
Every guy smells like what he is doin'."

"Yeah," Nutsie said, "and Mike and Paddy
O'Toole cleans all the backhouses in town for fifty
cents apiece, an' Christ only knows they smell like
what they been doin', too!"

"He-he-he-ha-ha-ha-ha-ha-haw-haw!" screamed
Wickie.

"Shut up! You goddam fool!" Cockie yelled
again.

"Well, someone has to clean 'em," Soapy said.

They walked down Perry Street, talking about
one thing and then another. Perry Street was
named for Perry Delaney and it celebrated him in
a proper way. It was a symbol. Perry was nearly
always drunk, and he had the red pimply nose you
used to see on a bar fly. The only thing that kept
Perry from being a bar fly was that his old man
had money. Anyway, that's what Soapy said.

All Old John's children had some peculiarity.
Clara, who married Henry Vance, lived on the
street named for her. People said that Henry married her for her money. And they said if he ever
got any of it he earned it. Clara's house was cluttered up like a pigpen. It smelled dirty. She always stayed in bed until noon. She kept a whole
flock of mangy-looking cats, and they were in

every corner of the house. They even crawled up on the table and licked the butter with their little red tongues. Old John had peculiar children. They were all slovenly, and they had money, too.

The gang went on down Perry Street to where it crossed Delaney Avenue. At the top of the De-laney Avenue hill and right across from the Scat-terfield graveyard they could see Lew Vortz's house. Lew was standing in his yellow front yard. He had his hands thrust deep in his pockets, and even from that distance it was easy to see that he was in his bare feet. Lew was a rivet bucker in a steel car company in the city, but he was laid off now for a week or more.

In the other direction they could see the dump. It was a quarter of a mile from Perry Street, but there was a slight breeze from down that way which carried the smell. Back of the dump and almost against the railroad tracks was the old shanty oc-cupied by Mike and Paddy O'Toole. The shanty had been built of every kind of old scrap lumber and from that distance resembled a crazy quilt. It wasn't high enough for a small boy to stand up in.

Mike and Paddy made a business of drinking rot-gut whisky, and fighting. As a side line they worked at cleaning outhouses and digging graves in the Scatterfield graveyard. They dug graves where worn-out human bodies were deposited in soggy clay, and they cursed and drank and fought while they worked.

"Tell you what," Nutsie said, "let's go up to Lew Vortz's place and see if he'll give us a glass of beer."

"Yeah," Soapy said, "but I don't want my old man to see me."

"It ain't time for your old man to be home yet, is it, Soapy?" Cockie asked.

"It ain't time, but you can't tell nothin' about him."

Soapy lived across the alley from Lew's place.

Nutsie liked beer. He drank it at home all the time, but he said Lew's beer was better because his old mother brewed it herself. The only beer Mark had ever tasted he got at Lew's. He didn't like it at first and drank it just to show he could, but he was used to the bitter taste now and it was good. Mark had to be careful. His mother never would have got over it if she had found it out. And maybe Michael would have tried to have Lew arrested.

"I'll go," Mark said, "if Soapy will swipe me some cloves for my breath."

"Lew'll give you some cloves," Nutsie said.

"No, he won't either," Mark replied. "And if he finds out I ain't allowed to drink it, he won't let me have it no more."

"That's right," Soapy agreed. "Come on. I'll git you some cloves when we come away."

So they all agreed on it and started up the hill.
Wickie came along, too. He always did.

When Lovett Smollett came driving Old John
Delaney's grocery wagon up that way, they piled
in the back end and rode. The horse hitched to the
wagon was not very prosperous-looking, but a fair
sample of the old man's stable. It was skinny, and
its head drooped. It was stringhalted and with every
other step lifted its hind legs clear to its belly.
Lovett used some vile language on that horse, but
it didn't do any good. The old nag had too much
actual abuse to become frightened at words.

Lovett was singing. He always sang between
curses. He sat so far back in the wagon that you
couldn't see him from the outside, and it sounded
a little ghostly sometimes to hear his thin, tenor
voice come floating out of that rattly old wagon.
He didn't pretend to see the gang when they
jumped on the end gate, but he knew they were
there. If Old John happened to see him hauling
a gang of ragamuffins around, Lovett would swear
he didn't know they were there.

The kids hopped out at Lew's house, and the old
wagon clattered and rattled on up the street. From
out of the clatter and noise Mark could distinguish
the song Lovett was singing: "In-the-shade-of-
the-old-apple-tree. . . !"

Lew was still standing in the front yard. It
didn't seem that he had moved an inch since they

started from the bottom of the hill. He was squeez-
ing the damp clay between his toes. He was a
powerfully built man. Just now he wore a blue
work shirt, open at the collar, exposing the matted
hair on his huge, thick chest. His sleeves were rolled
up to the elbow and his hands thrust idly into his
pockets. Above the elbow you could see the swell-
ing muscles outline themselves through the sleeves.
He had a beak nose and square jaws. His eyes were
small and black. They were angry-looking eyes
when they looked out at you from beneath his
heavy, frowning brow.

Lew lived there with his old mother, who spoke
only broken English, and Danny, his five-year-old
boy. The house was only one story high and had
only three rooms, but it looked like a house. The
paint was not more than two seasons old.

Danny was sitting on the front step. He was
a handsome little chap—though dirty most of the
time—and he had a sweet smile. He wore a little
suit of faded blue overalls which was caked with
yellow Scatterfield clay. He was learning fast there
in Scatterfield, and already knew how to swear
as well as a man. When he saw the Scatterfield
gang he smiled at them and shouted, "Hi there,
you! *Wie gehts?*" He always said *"Wie gehts?"*
and somehow that kind of greeting always made
everyone feel at home. It made you like Danny
right off.

"Lew," Nutsie said, "it's been so hot today we thought you might give us a glass of beer. What do you say, Lew? Ain't this good beer weather?"

Lew wasn't nearly so hard as he looked. He had a good heart: He said, "I just been thinkin' about beer myself. I hung a basket of it down in the well this morning. Sure, boys, we'll crack a bottle."

They all went around the house to the back door. Danny followed them. Lew's mother was pushing a wheelbarrow out of the chicken house. It was loaded with chicken manure. The German people in Scatterfield manured their gardens and made them produce. The old woman was fat. She wore a faded, calico dress that dragged on the ground, and the bottom of it had gathered a good deal of filth. Over the dress she had a checkered apron. It was dirty, too, and the strings were tied so tight around her thick waist that they dug a deep crevice in her body.

She had an old sunbonnet on her head which hid her wrinkled face, and her straggling hair swished about the bonnet like straw in a scarecrow's hat. There was a damp place on the belly part of her apron where she had been leaning against the kitchen sink washing dishes. She stopped the wheelbarrow every three or four feet and scattered the manure over the garden with a small fire shovel. When she labored forward again with her load, her fat belly jiggled like jelly.

Lew pulled up a basket of beer from the well
where it had been hanging to a rope. The bottles
were cold, and their brown surfaces were bright
and shining with a polish of well-water dripping
from them. You could see little particles of foam
in the bottle necks. The beer looked good to the
thirsty kids. Lew never allowed them to have more
than they could hold.

Danny always called his father Lew. Now he
said, "This is good beer weather, ain't it, Lew?"

"Sure is," Lew answered.

"Would you let me have a glass of it, Lew?"

"Yeah, I might let you have a little."

He gave Danny a little water glass half full, then
he gave each of the gang a big mug, and they dived
their noses deep into the foam. Lew set his mug
down and went over to the sink. He pumped a
basin of rain water and washed his face in it. When
his hands slid over his rough beard it sounded like
sandpaper.

"Them's fine whiskers you got, Lew," Danny
said.

"Sure are," Lew acknowledged. Then he came
back and sat down between the stove and the sink.

The inside of Lew's kitchen was battered up,
and there was no covering on the floor. The table
didn't even have a piece of oilcloth on it. It was
covered with grease. It was comfortable just the

same—to sit there and drink beer. That's what Mark thought, anyway.

There were three or four scarred straight-back chairs and an old rocker. The rocking chair had had one rocker broken, which Lew had mended with pieces of lath. Many summer evenings the people of Scatterfield had heard the old woman singing German lullabies while she rocked Danny to sleep in that chair. The mended place in the rocker clanked and thumped, and the old woman's quavering voice rolled out through the gathering dusk. When she would get Danny to sleep she would put him into bed without washing his dirty feet. Then she and Lew would sit about in the kitchen drinking beer.

Lew read a good bit. There was a row of big-looking books placed on the shelf back of the stove. They were greasy-looking, too. The title of one of them was *Das Kapital,* by Karl Marx. Mark always remembered that one because Lew talked about Marx so much. He almost worshipped Marx. That was the reason why J. Wellingsford Knowles claimed Lew was a public menace. The title of the book was stamped in gold, but the lettering was almost covered over with grease and dirt.

Nutsie and Cockie and Wickie all left ahead of Mark and Soapy. Mark wanted to wait for Soapy, because Soapy was going to get him some cloves for his beer breath. He would get them from his

mother. She didn't care how much beer either of
them drank. She was good enough to Soapy, but
his old man beat him hard sometimes.

The two kids liked to hear Lew talk anyway. He
talked to them about Socialism. And there was a
wonder in his voice. It was deep and mighty, and
it rolled in the air like great waves on the ocean.
Most people listened to him, whether they believed
in what he was saying or not. Sometimes he stumbled a little and groped for words, and his hands
would sweep about wildly as though he were trying
to grab his words out of the air.

Soapy and Mark sat there sort of charmed by
his voice until finally something broke the charm.
Soapy jumped up quickly and looked out the back
door. Soapy's father came driving in the back
alley in his junk wagon. He saw Soapy, too. He
stopped at his barn and climbed down from beneath the great umbrella atop the wagon seat.

Old Dick Pendleton was an inoffensive-looking
man, but Mark had seen him trounce Soapy before.
He always did a thorough job of it. Dick's face
was lean and long. His eyes sagged like those of a
hound dog, and the lower lids looked as if they had
turned wrong side out. They looked like raw
wounds. His long untrimmed mustache drooped
clear to his chin, covering his mouth completely.
He always talked slow and easy, but that way of

talking was often a fooler. He saw Soapy and called to him.

"S-o-a-p-y," he said.

He said it very slowly, and you expected him to put his arm around the boy's shoulder and get chummy. But Soapy knew what to expect, and he knew he couldn't dodge it like he dodged soap and rain water. Soapy went out Lew's back door and approached Old Dick's wagon just like a dog does when he expects to get a beating. When he got out to the wagon, Dick spoke to him again.

"S-o-a-p-y," he said. "I-thought-I-told-you-to-cut-up-that-wood."

And while he said it he hauled off and hit Soapy on the jaw with his fist. Mark could hear the loud crack from where he stood. He hit him just as hard as he would have hit a man.

Old Pendleton's fist landed on the side of Soapy's jaw where the big cud of tobacco stayed, and it left the jaw just as flat as a pancake. Soapy lit in the manure pile and sunk into it like he had been shot out of a cannon. He grabbed his jaw and began to spit tobacco juice and blood.

He lay there looking at his old man—like a cornered rat watches a dog—without saying a word. He didn't even attempt to get up until his father walked around the wagon and was at a safe distance.

Then Soapy got up and went around the corner of the barn, still holding his jaw.

"Jeeezuss!" Lew said.

"There goes my cloves," Mark blurted.

"What cloves?" asked Lew.

"Oh!—nothin', Lew," Mark answered. "But it's time for me to be a-goin' or I'll git lammed, too."

Mark hiked out for home, but he was scared. He went in the kitchen door and grabbed the milk buckets.

"Where've you been?" Judy asked suspiciously.

"Down the creek—fishin'," he answered hurriedly.

Then he hiked out to the barn before she got a chance to ask him anything else. He took a long time to milk, and when he came back in supper was ready. He didn't say much. He was afraid Michael would smell his breath. He wouldn't mind the whipping so much as he would the chance of getting someone else in trouble for giving it to him.

He sneaked off to bed right after supper. They never suspected. He stopped up the crack under his door and lit a cigarette. After he had smoked it he lit his lamp and read some of Dick Merriwell's adventures.

But that was just one day in Scatterfield. It was one day that Mark Cullen always remembered —even though all days are different. There was a bright June sun over Scatterfield that day, and spring was late. . . .

July is usually a pretty dry month in Ohio. Sometimes it is that way in June. If the dry spell lasts long, great cracks open in the earth, and the sun's terrific heat sucks out precious moisture. Often the wheat is blasted, and all the crops are short.

Farmers keep cultivators scraping through their fields in a frantic effort to keep a dust mulch over the surface of the soil so that the moisture may be preserved for the roots. And they look often at the sky. They explore the whole domed roof of the world for signs of rain. Hopefully they watch each lazy patch of white floating serenely above them, and they talk constantly of the weather. They hope it will rain soon, they say. And the wish is repeated so often that it becomes almost a prayer.

It was such a July in Scatterfield that year. But the Scatterfield folk wanted rain for another reason save that of restoring crops. They thought of the crops, but they wanted more than anything a cool retreat. The insides of their battered hovels were like ovens, and there was little shade out of doors.

At evening they sat in desolate yards, watching the big, red sun drop below the horizon. They watched with grateful eyes the dark curtain of night swing cautiously over them. Morning found them crawling out into the still, hot air like insects.

Only that Scatterfield gang found relief from the heat. They ran like naked Indians about the bottoms along Yellow Creek, and they swam for hours at a time.

Soap Dodger Pendleton and Mark Cullen had been sleeping in the ravine off Delaney Avenue at night. Judy had agreed to it. It was so hot in the house, she told Michael. And Michael grumbled and agreed. It was cool there in the valley, and the boys slept soundly.

It was like being far from the world of men, down in that ravine at night, and you couldn't believe that Scatterfield lay beyond the hill. The slopes above the kids caught the noise of the town and banked it. Now and then they could hear a door slam, or a kid yammering, but the sound was faint and almost pleasant.

When night dropped over the valley, the place seemed strange. In darkness it didn't look familiar. The bushes and trees along the brook were like great rolled clouds, banked in blackness. They were phantomlike, and if you looked at them very long, they vanished. They just became a part of the night. But you could look away a moment, and when you looked back they were there again.

The kids got their blankets out early. They stretched themselves out and watched the darkness drop slowly over them. Darkness comes that way in summer. Tired and indifferent. They could see everything about them at first, but in a little while the scuffed places and worn paths on the hillside turned dark, and leaves on bushes and trees dissolved into rolled green patches.

They lay on their backs and looked into the darkening sky. In a little while a single star blinked above them. Then there were two and three. And in no time at all there were a million of them. The frogs croaked mournfully along the brook, and the sad voices of insects ripped through the wall of darkness. Everything changed in that short time. The whole world. The kids undressed and crawled into the blankets. The air was cool.

"That there sky is purty at night, hain't it, Mark?" Soapy said. Soapy didn't often talk like that. Mark was always cautious about saying anything was pretty. Soapy usually sneered at pretty things.

"Yeah," Mark answered. "It sure is."

"Old Charlie Heston says that them there stars is awful fur from here," Soapy continued. "He says that you couldn't git the figger into a book. He says that when you say how fur a star is, you say it in years instead of miles."

"Yeah, I heard him say that. It's right, I guess. Charlie knows all about the stars."

"Charlie'd ort to know," Soapy said. "He used ta teach about the stars in college. He's smart."

"Yeah," Mark agreed. "Did he ever let you look through that there telescope of his'n that he sets up on his shanty roof sometimes?"

"Yeah, he showed me the moon through it. The moon sure looks funny through that thing."

But Soapy didn't stay on the subject of astronomy very long. He jumped right into another subject that had lately intrigued his wayward fancy. It was a pretty mysterious subject and often sent Mark's head to reeling, too.

"I wonder what ol' Flossie Kershner's a-doin'," Soapy said. And his words were full of dark meaning.

"She's prob'ly makin' her ol' man hump it up," Mark replied.

"Jesus," Soapy said. "I wish't it was me."

The subject set Mark's head whirling, and his heart throbbed. He always tried not to think of it. For there had been dark and secret acts in that boy's life which left a long, black trail of shame over his conscience. They left him with a sense of sin and sent his brain to shuddering with the weight of it. But to think of Flossie now was exciting, and Mark wanted to talk about her.

"I bet she'd be good at it, all right," he ventured, trembling with thought.

"Why, I'll say she would," Soapy agreed enthusiastically. "Why, she loves it. An' they always say she likes kids better'n men."

"She sure likes you, Soapy," Mark said. " 'Cause she always speaks to ya, even if they's more of us there. She'll be callin' ya in some of these days."

"Naw, she don't like me no more'n other kids. She's jist got a eye for kids—when they git 'bout our age."

They fell into silence, but sleep would not come to Mark. He kept thinking of Flossie—of her body. He visualized her heavy breasts, and he could almost see the white valley softly creviced between them. Mark had seen pictures of partly nude women. His eyes took them in hungrily in Latherup Jones's barber shop. And the sense of sin was heavy upon him after each visit there.

Mark lay tense and motionless for a long time. Ridges in the hard earth beneath him bored into his back, and his eyes were too tightly closed for sleep. Presently he glanced at Soapy, who appeared to be asleep. Then he crept stealthily out of the blankets and climbed the worn path beyond the brook. He parted a clump of bushes and stepped into them.

"Where ya been?" Soapy asked when Mark returned. Mark was prepared for the question.

"I jist went up the hill a way and took a leak," he said.

"I guess I will, too," Soapy said, crawling out of the blankets.

Mark felt desolate and ashamed and alone. He whipped his conscience with the lash of thought, and told himself he was unworthy of human companionship. His mind pleaded for sleep, so that

thought might not longer torture him. But now
he suspected Soapy, and that suspicion salved his
conscience—if only a little. Morning would sweep
the evil from his mind. Soapy came back and
crawled silently into the blankets.

Music from a guitar came softly over the hill
and drifted into the valley. Swede Olson sitting
on his back porch in Ohio's summer night. Swede,
sitting in a hard, straight-back chair, with his feet
propped against the porch rail. Looking at the
night and playing a tune about it.

The music was like the night. It was low and
uncertain. It mingled with the darkness and the
voices of insects and frogs. It mingled with everything. You couldn't tell what it said. But you
knew it was saying that same thing that all night
voices were saying. It belonged to the night. It
was part of the night. Mark felt a little better after
that music, and he fell asleep.

Soapy and Mark rounded up the rest of the gang
in the morning. That is—they got Cockie and
Nutsie. Wickie was waiting for Soapy when he
got home from the ravine. He always was. The
kids started walking aimlessly out Delaney Avenue,
knowing all the time that they would eventually
get to Yellow Creek.

They headed for John Delaney's apple orchard,

and before they reached it, they could see Flossie Kershner sitting silently on her front steps. Nutsie giggled.

"There's Flossie a-waitin' fer ya, Soapy," he said.

"Aw, hell!" Soapy answered. "She hain't a-waitin' fer me."

"The way she looks at ya, she's already got ya a-humpin'," Nutsie said. And all the kids laughed.

Flossie watched the gang approach her. You could tell she wasn't very young. Her face was seamed with wrinkles—perhaps prematurely—and the dark pouches under her eyes looked like rotten mushrooms. Strands of stringy brown hair lay about her face, like the locks of Medusa. But there was something darkly suggestive about her body. She wore a house dress drawn tightly about her round hips, and you could see her yellow stockings to the knee.

Her eyes were hungry. Something as old as life looked out of those green eyes. She spoke to Soapy, and her eyes caressed his slender body.

"Hello, Soapy," she said. "Where you boys a-goin' today?"

Her words were smooth and soft. The kids felt them, almost, as they tumbled about in their minds. Flossie was like that. She looked hungrily at kids who were clutching at the thin strands of manhood.

"Swimmin', I guess," Soapy answered.

The kids just kept walking. None of them said anything. Wickie got excited. He panted hoarsely, and drool frothed his wide lips.

When they got out of the range of her moderate voice, the kids crossed Delaney Avenue and climbed a short slope into the orchard. The sun was mounting the sky, and already the kids were hot. They giggled about Soapy and Flossie and kidded him for a long time.

Everybody in Scatterfield talked about Flossie. They knew all about her hungry appetites. They talked and talked; but they laughed, too. It wasn't anything serious, they thought. Most of the Scatterfield folk were sorry for Flossie's one-eyed husband. Old Sip Kershner dragging his weary feet over that town's cinder paths to the car line and back each day. Working hard in a factory while Flossie two-timed him and drained his feeble strength. People called him "Sip" because he had a mouth like a Mississippi catfish.

But when people said they felt sorry for old Sip, they laughed meaningly. He was thin and drawn and tired-looking. In his scrawny hand he always carried a tin dinner pail. He held it with such tired indifference that it resembled a burden. He must have known about Flossie, though. Everyone else did. Soapy said he thought Sip was glad when someone else did come in to help him with Flossie.

Soapy said that she was just too damned much for one man to handle.

The sun dripped through the diseased leaves on the apple trees in the orchard and dropped a mottled network of shadows over the kids as they walked. They felt pretty wicked—and pretty grown up, too—talking about Flossie Kershner.

"What'll ya do, Soapy," Nutsie asked, "when Flossie calls ya in ta fix 'er kitchen sink?"

"Well, I reckon I can fix 'er goddam sink," Soapy boasted.

"She's sure got a eye fer ya, Soapy," Cockie giggled.

"Aw!" Soapy hollered. "That's jist a tale they tell about her. She don't wanna monkey with no kids."

When the kids got back to the end of the orchard, they forgot Flossie. They slipped into a new vein of conversation easily, like all kids do.

The ground dropped a little back there, and you couldn't see Scatterfield after you had passed over a little knoll. The orchard opened into a little gully so that you could see the place where Hump Bing's cabin used to stand. But that was long ago, and Hump was in the penitentiary, now. The cabin was burned to the ground, and you had to look close to see traces of it at all.

On the opposite side of the gully there was a barbed-wire fence, and beyond it a field of tall corn.

The green stalks drooped their tasseled heads under the withering sun. It was only field corn, but the gang had made a good many round meals of it. They didn't steal any of it that day, though, because they didn't want to carry it all the way to Yellow Creek. The fence marked the end of John Delaney's property.

They climbed the fence and plunged into the corn. They went on through the field and into Hacket's road. Then they followed the road to the creek.

The corn in the bottoms along Yellow Creek was tall, too, and the kids stripped off their clothing and hid it far back between the rows. Then they ran along the creek naked. They poured water over a mud slide and scooted over it into the water. Once in a while they would plaster their bodies with mud and bake in the sun before plunging in. It was pleasant to feel the dry mud soften in the water, and lose its grip on their bodies.

After a while they swiped corn from the field and caught a mess of crawfish. They ate only the tails of the crawfish. They had a few frogs, too. They mud roasted the corn and cooked the meat on hot rocks. They lay about in the shade after the meal.

Soapy's lean and stringy muscles were getting to look more and more like those of a man. He looked like a little half-formed man. His shoulders were broadening out, too.

"You're gettin' a lot of hair on ya, hain't ya, Soapy?" Cockie said. He spoke very gravely.

"Yeah," Soapy said.

All the kids looked at their bodies. Hair was springing from their flesh like frail spring grass in a seeded plot. Mark was a little embarrassed—not because of what they were saying—but because he was afraid their words would bring their attention to his skinniness. His ribs traced themselves through his flesh plainly, and his arms and legs were thin. He was nearly as thin as Wickie, he thought, except that his hands and feet were smaller.

"You got more hair on ya than any of us, hain't ya, Soapy?" Nutsie observed.

"Yeah," Soapy said proudly, "I got lotsa hair. I'm a hairy son of a bitch."

Back in John Delaney's apple orchard, the kids picked wormy apples. They lay in the sparse shade, overlooking Delaney Avenue. The street stretched out below them. They could look down the slope and far down the street. They sprawled there, filling their bellies with green apples.

Mark sat with his back propped against a tree trunk. The air was so hot that his breath was warm in his nostrils. Even the breeze felt warm to his face. And the sunlight, puncturing the stingy leaves above the kids, punished their bodies. The leaves were coated with a heavy film of yellow dust which floated always from the street below. On the far hillside, the green of spring lay helplessly in brown death.

Houses along the street were without shade. They cringed in the bright sunlight. Far over on Perry Street waves of heat danced madly atop Limpy Peters' drugstore. Teams of horses plodding slowly toward Old John's lumberyard, left clouds of dust trailing languidly after them. And Old John's grocery wagon clattered up the street with side curtains flapping in the breeze. The dust in its wake rolled lazily toward the orchard, too.

Mark got to thinking of winter. It was hard to believe that winter ever would come again to Scatterfield. He said that to Soapy.

"It's hard to think of winter on a hot day like this, hain't it, Soapy?" he said. "It's hard ta believe they is such a thing as winter."

"I don't never think nothing about it," Soapy answered.

None of the other kids were thinking about it, either. It was that time of day when conversation is exhausted—that time of day when you realize that plans have failed. Unless, maybe, something happened to make the day a success. It was late afternoon. Mark, glancing at Soapy, could see plainly enough that he had his eyes on Flossie Kershner.

Flossie had moved her chair from the blistering heat and now sat in the shade beside the house. The house was a dismal shack; not much more. It had no foundation, and the weather-beaten clapboard siding had never been painted. The boards were grey with age. Their ends were jagged with dry rot and met the earth beneath like snag teeth. The house leaned anxiously backward, propping itself against a lean-to kitchen. The two structures appeared to be holding each other upright.

Flossie sat motionless as before, looking silently at everything and thinking her own thoughts. You only suspected what Flossie was thinking when her greedy green eyes devoured you.

Some of the Scatterfield men were coming home, now, from their work in the city. They trooped down the paths along the street, their weary feet crunching the cinders. They walked in groups of two or three or four—or walked tired and alone. Work shirts were opened at collars, and sleeves were rolled at elbows. Armpits were patched with dark sweat stains. Some shouldered coats and carried dinner pails. Their hollow voices floated up the hillside in a wordless mumble.

Nutsie Doane rolled a cigarette. He used the last of his tobacco and tossed the empty can down the slope before him. It clattered and tumbled and came to a stop halfway down. He lit the cigarette and locked his arms about his knees. He squinted his eye, so that the thin stream of blue smoke ascending his cheek rolled over it without pain. He inhaled and blew the smoke from his lungs in a straight, heavy stream. You could tell he knew how to smoke. Cockie watched him hungrily.

"Gimme the willies on that cigarette, will you, Nutsie?" Cockie said finally.

Nutsie grunted—kept smoking. Soapy lay on his belly and watched Flossie. He was clean from his bath in the creek. His legs were plastered with mud, though, from wading in muddy water for crawfish. Wickie panted like a dog. Nutsie got up, finally.

"I gotta git home," he announced, "or I'll catch hell."

"I gotta go, too," Cockie said, "I'm hungry."

Wickie jumped up nervously and followed them down the slope. Soapy and Mark watched them idly. Cockie reached out his hand again to Nutsie.

"Hey!" he hollered, "Gimme the willies on that snipe, will ya? Before it's all gone."

Nutsie inhaled again and handed him the cigarette. It was nearly burned up. Cockie cupped his fingers about it and held it to his lips. He breathed the smoke hungrily into his lungs, and it poured from his nostrils with each breath. Then he handed it to Wickie. Wickie sucked on it a few times and tossed it away.

Soapy and Mark watched them until their voices got to be an uneven mumble. At the bottom of the slope a thin stream of smoke from the cigarette ascended feebly, and dissipated itself in the warm air.

"I gotta go, too, Soapy," Mark said. "It's gittin' suppertime."

"Yeah," Soapy answered, still looking at Flossie Kershner's shack. "I have, too. I'll be like to git a beatin' now. The old man said I had ta hoe the pertaters, an' I never done it. To hell with his goddam pertaters. I never planted the stuff."

Flossie stood in her front doorway as they walked by her house. She was just inside the screen door, looking out. A large rent in the bottom of the screen opened a passage for swarms of lazy flies. Flossie leaned on the door frame, so that her dress dropped carelessly over her hips. Mark's throat tightened when he looked at them.

"Hi!" Soapy called.

"Say, Soapy," she said. "Come here a minute. I want to tell you something."

Soapy went up to the door, and Flossie said something to him in a low voice. Mark couldn't hear them. In just a moment, Soapy was back.

"What did she want?" Mark asked. "Did she want ya to hump fer her? Jesus, did she, Soapy?"

Soapy looked wise and shook his head.

"Naw!" he said. "She jist wanted me to tell my old man to pick up some junk there at her house."

"You're a awful liar, Soapy," Mark grinned.

Soapy grinned, too, and the pair of them felt like they were men. But Mark didn't say anything more.

Mark couldn't get Flossie and Soapy out of his mind. He thought of them all morning, as he worked in Michael's garden. He got through with his assigned work at noon. After dinner he started to hunt for Soapy. He couldn't find any of the gang. He looked through all the orchard and wandered about in the lumberyard and finally went to the creek. A group of other kids were at the creek, but none of the gang.

He walked up the creek bank to the ford and sat alone on the bank. He felt lazy and tired. Looking out over the water, his mind drifted, like it does when energy has been spent. He didn't think of anything and was only vaguely conscious of the sunlight dancing on the water before him. The water made a gurgling noise as it poured over green-looking rocks, but even that sound drifted away from him. He lost all sense of time and place.

He fastened his eyes in a dull stare on the opposite creek bank. It was lined with little clusters of willows, and the ends of their branches drooped in the water. Little whirlpools tore with impotent fury at the ends, drawing them downstream and releasing them to fly back and be drawn in again. The motion was constant, like a curious game.

Just staring at the willows brought dots before Mark's eyes. When the dots came, the bushes receded. The dots raced toward a common center and became a pinpoint hole that drew his eyes toward it. It was like having one eye in the center of his head. Staring that way he could see only one branch of the willow, sweeping back and forth in the water. It seemed miles away.

It was like a trance, and Mark came out of it lazily. The faint gurgling of water grew louder and the pinpoint hole widened. The dots returned to race before his eyes. Then they vanished, and the whole creek bed lay before him again.

He was conscious again, of the heat—and he was tired. He lay back and closed his eyes. The sun bored into the closed lids. His eyes looked into the lids. They were like a dark wall, over which colors rolled in blanketed waves. The colors were mostly green and purple and dark red. Some of them were tinged with yellow.

Mark sat up suddenly, thinking of Soapy—wondering where that dirty kid had gone. He leaped up, then, for he was certain he knew. He hastened back Hacket's road and ran through the cornfield. He raced through the orchard and brought up at the top of the slope overlooking Delaney Avenue.

As he watched Flossie Kershner's house, nervous desire pulsed through his body in hot waves. Her chair was vacant, and she was not within the range

of his vision. He could see the screen door, bulged
and warped by pushing hands, but nothing about
the place moved. It stood silent and deserted. Mark
almost knew what was going on in there.

He gave a sudden start when he heard Flossie's
back door bang. And there he was. There was
Soapy, sneaking like a guilty dog up the alley. He
disappeared in Delaney's lumberyard.

A picture, clear and distinct, raced through
Mark's mind. He saw what had happened in Flossie's house, and it sent through his body a fire
which he could not control. His heart pounded,
and emotion stifled his breath. It grew in volume
until he had to get up from the ground. He wondered how much of her body Soapy had seen.
Mark's trembling legs carried him down the slope
and into Delaney Avenue. With no sense of direction, his footsteps followed habit. He walked toward home.

Dark and overpowering, Mark Cullen fought
blindly at the passion surging through him. He
fought as all boys fight, without the discretion of
manhood to strengthen him.

He saw Michael working in the garden, but
walked straight to the barn. There he bridled the
horse and led him into the alley. He leaped on his
back and gave the animal a sharp slap with the
reins. The horse snorted and leaped into a furious
gallop.

Swinging down Sunset Drive and past the town dump, he forgot Flossie for only a moment. For that brief moment he was Jesse James riding over the unbroken plain. Beyond the dump, he jumped the horse across a ditch. The animal stumbled and nearly fell, but leaped forward again under the smarting reins.

He rode the horse through an open field and passed Old John's worn and weather-beaten sign which admonished workers to buy a lot and own their own homes. Then he galloped the horse into the orchard and toward Delaney Avenue. He'll show Flossie Kershner how he could ride—even if he was skinny.

The horse's sides were heaving with painful gasps of breath, and he snorted froth from his mouth. Sweat on the animal's back had lathered into white, foamy ridges. He would show Flossie that he could sit on a horse's back in the same way that he sat in a rocking chair. Somehow Mark thought this would prove something to Flossie. It would prove that he might be a sturdy kid himself.

But Flossie wasn't interested. She watched casually as Mark clattered by her house in a cloud of dust. She didn't move and she didn't wave.

"Hell," Mark thought bitterly. "She probably thinks I'm crazy—ridin' a horse that hard on a hot day. And what would she want of a skinny runt like me?"

He rode back home, and as he entered the gate, he leaped to the ground. He led the horse to the watering trough. Michael ran toward him from the garden. His features were full of anger. He clutched the reins and shouted.

"You danged little fool!" he hollered. "You've got him all in a lather! What the devil's the matter with you? Are you crazy?"

He fetched Mark with a resounding clip on the ear. The boy dodged, cut the corner of the house, and raced into the street. Looking back, he saw Michael leading the horse into the barn. Mark stopped running and tried to bring back his scattered faculties. His hands trembled violently.

He walked far out through the orchard and down through the gully. Climbing the fence, he walked slowly into the cornfield. Far back in the wilderness of green cornstalks, he threw himself to the ground. He was exhausted, and his legs felt weak. The earth beneath his body had been ridged with cultivator teeth, but it was soft and pleasant. He scooped a layer of dusty topsoil away and thrust his hot, sweaty cheek into the cool subsoil.

With his head thrust to one side, he could see the roots to a cornstalk. They were like a spider. Against one of them lay a tiny, husklike splinter, and Mark dug with his finger at the earth, tracing the root. It burrowed its way into the soil, and beneath the surface it was covered with scores of tendrillike subroots. Curious, he thought, that such frail tendrils could nourish the whole stalk—could give it life and the power to grow.

Mark felt restful, now, and the dark, sallow features of Flossie Kershner vanished from his mind. He got to thinking of something Charlie Heston had told him. Charlie had said that some men feel a deep kinship for the soil; that the soil is a part of their being. He said that Michael was that kind of a man. He tilled the soil, Charlie said, with an emotion resembling love. But he said that Michael was not conscious of it.

Now Mark sifted the dust through his fingers. It was like dry sand, and his nostrils picked up the musty, earthy smell of the moist soil beneath. He now remembered the old house—remembered the first time he had ever watched soil being prepared for planting. He was conscious of that odor then. He had liked it, and he liked it now. No odor on earth could please his senses so much, he thought.

He stretched his arms and legs in a clutching gesture as though he were about to embrace the earth. Maybe he was beginning to understand what Charlie Heston had said.

Lying with Soapy under a blanket in the dark ravine that night, Mark heard the story of Soapy's first adventure with a woman. Mark dug at the details, trying to piece together the mystery of it —trying to understand, as Soapy himself tried to understand. Older people do not help the young with such matters. Boys stumble over the brink of manhood, pick up the ends of a sorry puzzle, and work at it for years. Then they lay the puzzle aside unsolved and accept things as they are.

Soapy bragged a good deal, adding here and there a few spicy touches. But he, himself, was puzzled about part of his adventure, just as Mark was puzzled. He told Mark he didn't understand it. It is a thing which visits the very young after a casual adventure with a woman.

"Afterwards," Soapy said, in a voice that revealed how really puzzled he was. "Afterwards I felt like I wanted to wash her off'n me."

It sounded a little ridiculous to Mark, because Soapy was such a dirty kid.

"You know what I done?" he resumed. "Well, sir, I went home and took a bath in the washtub."

"She must of been awful dirty if ya felt like that," Mark ventured. Then Mark lay quietly, waiting for Soapy to go on with the story—if there was any more to it.

"Well," Soapy concluded. "I guess I'm a man now, sure enough."

Music from Swede Olson's guitar came softly over the hill and sifted itself into the night. It was soft and low and became a part of all night sounds. That Swede Olson certainly could play a tune about the night.

Soapy and Mark were silent, now. Mark never knew what Soapy was thinking. But he learned that in the days that followed, Soapy often visited Flossie. Finally Soapy spoke to him again.

"Say, Mark," he urged. "Don't never tell no one about it, will ya. I don't care, only they'd sure enough send me to Reform School if anybody'd git to know. Don't even tell Nutsie or Cockie or any of them guys, will ya?"

"No. I won't never tell nobody."

The kids stopped talking then, and Mark got to thinking of himself lying far back in the cornfield and sifting dusty earth between his fingers. Wondering what really makes corn grow. Music. Music and the night. That Swede Olson certainly could play a guitar.

It was autumn again in Scatterfield. More than half of October had been spent. The first half of the month had been nice. There had been warm clear days and cool nights. Bits of color showed up brightly against the yellow hills. It had been like Indian Summer. But now it rained incessantly, and the yellow dusty streets were thick and sticky with mud. The sky was a thick, grey blanket that hooded the world, and midday was like dusk.

Four walls of a battered old schoolroom held the Scatterfield gang now—day in and day out. The kids sat through long, tedious hours slumped in their seats; thinking of nothing at all. They stared at their books without seeing the printed page, or they saw the pages blurred and without meaning.

The old jacketed stove sagged heavily in the middle of the room, and rows and rows of desks divided themselves there. A marble dropped in one corner of the room would have rolled to the center.

Wickie Winters sat next to Mark Cullen. He already had his seasonal cold, and his flabby upper lip was slimy with a coating of frost. The goose flesh on his lean chest and belly showed through where several buttons were missing on his waist. He was barefooted and wore no underwear. Now, he was amusing himself by running a safety-pin point through the upper part of his fingernails. His hands were filthy and damp with nervous sweat. He watched the process eagerly, and his Simian features were aflame with delight.

Wickie's mother washed for the more affluent families in Scatterfield. His father had been killed several years before in a drunken brawl. Most people in Scatterfield washed for themselves, and Wickie's mother did not make a good living. Wickie was very little help to her. He just couldn't seem to think of things.

Soap Dodger Pendleton sat to Mark's right and two seats back. He fashioned tiny javelins from matches and pins and hurled them cunningly at the back of Harold Knowles's head. His aim was generally good, and from time to time Harold was forced to pull a quarter of an inch of pin from his head. He would look at Soapy indignantly but always found him studying his geography intently.

None of the gang liked Harold, and he was the brunt of a good many practical jokes. He got his lessons too well to please any of them, and he was a tattletale and teacher's pet. Soapy couldn't chew his great cud of tobacco in the schoolroom but kept his lower lip lined with scrap. It satisfied him in a halfway manner, he said. It brought forth very little juice, and what it did bring forth Soapy swallowed.

Cockie Werner sat in the last seat in the last row to the left. He kept his big geography upright on his desk, and inside the covers he concealed a Diamond Dick novel. He read the dreary hours away.

And Nutsie Doane with his crooked arm was never in that Scatterfield school. He went to Catholic school in the city.

The girls in the Scatterfield school bore the marks of poverty with patience. Many of them looked thin and wasted. Their eyes were dull, and they seemed old beyond their years. They drudged many hours each morning before school in poverty-ridden kitchens. They waited through long school hours until time to go home and work again. Only Margaret Castell was plump and indolent. She was the

daughter of Old Farmer Castell and had been fat-
tened on roast chicken, fine ham, buckwheat cakes,
and homemade bread. She never worked at home,
for her mother kept a hired girl for that.

Mr. Light taught them reading, writing, arithmetic, history, and geography. They listened abstractedly to his monotonous voice. He repeated
word for word what he had said last year and the
year before. Teaching was a habit, and he didn't
have to think what he said.

When he taught history, he spoke of dates and
events which must be catalogued and stored side
by side in the mind. There were rules in history
and geography, just as in arithmetic and language.

While Mr. Light spewed out his stock of knowledge, he dreamed of his native village nestled back
in the mountains of Vermont. He was about forty,
now, and thought of his life as a thing wasted. He
sometimes spoke of himself as a man of capabilities,
wasting his talents in Scatterfield.

In ordinary weather Old Light sat all day at his
desk and talked monotonously. He kept his pudgy
hands folded across the desk top before him. But
in the rainy season he grew restless. He stood before
his desk and gazed across the room to the back
windows, where the rain beat ceaselessly against the
panes. He looked far beyond to the yellow hills
exposing their indecent nakedness to the wind and
rain—to the hovels and shacks dotting the hills like

age-old wounds, refusing to heal. Mr. Light would wrinkle his brow in a pathetic gesture of despair.

Sometimes he walked furiously back and forth before his desk, biting his upper lip with his lower teeth. And he talked of the Vermont woods—of his old home. He talked of the mountains, and of the deep, white, winter snow that seemed to spread itself over the whole world. His voice was bitter, and harsh lines ran through his face. He clasped his hands behind him and talked as though he were arguing with someone.

"Life there was a beautiful thing," he would say. "It was not like this God-forsaken place. Maybe it was because I was young, though. Maybe it was because I was young and expected so much from life. But, no. It was better than this."

When he spoke of Vermont that way the kids listened attentively. It was respite from monotony and boredom. It made Vermont seem like a real place. But when Mr. Light taught about the State of Vermont in geography lesson, it seemed a very remote place, if it existed at all. The same was true of all the countries of Europe, of South America, and of Africa. They were countries noted for this and for that. They imported certain things and exported others. But they did not really exist, except to disturb the minds of children. And the kids sat through an eternity of time until the teacher jangled a little bell on his desk, dismissing school for the day.

Mark never again wanted to draw near to Mary Hartman. He avoided her. Yet, in his curious boy mind, he felt ashamed of his weakness. Mary had offended his sensibilities without meaning to. But she had blasted a dreamland he had carefully built. She had brought him from the clouds and placed his feet upon the ground. Hers was a first lesson, and he never forgot it. When he grew older he developed more understanding—more sympathy. In later years he tried always to see the world as it was. He turned aside every impulse that might have made him successful in this curious world. He turned them aside because they appeared to guide him into error. And he never forgot Mary Hartman, who taught him a first lesson in realism.

But that autumn in Scatterfield the gang had another geography teacher, and one who had no formal education or connection with the school.

His name was Nat Briggs, and he had only lived in Scatterfield about a year. He said he never stayed in one place very long at a time. He was a drifter and a 'bo. Nat had been most every place in the kids' geography textbook, and he liked to tell about it. The gang liked to listen. Mark suspected that part of his stories were lies, but they were high-sounding lies and told skillfully. Mark liked to hear him talk.

It was Friday and had been raining the whole week. It hadn't let up more than fifteen minutes at a time and had rained hard. When school let out that day the gang walked out the cinder path together.

"It's still rainin' like all billy-be-damned and there hain't no place else ta go," Soapy said. "Let's go up and talk to Nat."

"I can't go," Cockie said. "I got to git home an' git my work done or I'll git a damned good whalin'."

And you knew that Cockie had had a recent beating or he wouldn't have considered the possibility. Mark hadn't had one in a long time. It didn't take him long to agree.

"Sure, Soapy, I'll go with you," Mark said.

That settled it. Soapy and Mark went up. Wickie never had to worry about a whipping at home. It wouldn't have bothered him anyway. He went along, but he never counted for much.

The kids went down Delaney Avenue and crossed the tottery old bridge spanning the brook. The brook was out of banks, and the coffee-colored water foamed and rushed madly through the valley. Mark had on rubber boots, and he splashed about joyously in the muddy streets. Soapy had on a pair of his father's cast-off hobnail shoes. They were many sizes too large for him, and as he walked, little streams of water oozed out of them. His black stockings had several large holes in them which exposed big spots of dirty underwear. The bottoms of his cheap knickerbockers were unbuckled and hung haphazard. They were frayed and nearly reached his ankles.

Wickie's bare feet were blue with cold, but he didn't mind. He walked along with Mark and Soapy, laughing inanely at nothing at all. When he laughed his ugly mouth spread wide.

Nat Briggs lived in a back alley at the rear of Old John Delaney's lumberyard. He lived in a little shanty that was only large enough for a sleeping cot and a small stove.

The boys cut through the side alley and past Old John's stables. Several teamsters were unhitching their horses there in the rain. Jake Redman was one of them. When the boys passed him he pointed to Wickie and grinned. He exposed a row of uneven yellow teeth.

"What the hell you two kids got with ya, a boy, or a monkey?" he shouted. "It hain't nothin' human, is it?"

Wickie didn't know very much, but he always knew when people were making fun of him. He jumped and jiggled about, now, in a furious rage. He looked like a person with Saint Vitus's dance. He frothed at the mouth and snarled and screamed. Finally he reached to the ground and picked up a big stone. He hurled it at Jake with all his strength.

Jake dodged just in time, but the stone struck one of the bony nags full in the flank. Jake didn't have any more time to look at Wickie for a while. He had all he could do to quiet the horse. It had got tangled in the traces, and it kicked about frantically for a time. Jake finally got the horse quiet, and he turned around and looked again toward Wickie. His grin was gone.

"You goddam crazy little bastard," he howled. "What the hell did you do that for?"

Wickie was pleased. He danced about and stuck out his long, red tongue. It lay quietly between his wide, flabby lips. It wasn't pretty. Then Wickie laughed.

"He-he-he-ha-ha-ha-ha-haw-haw!"

"Serves you right," Soapy said.

Wickie walked on with the two boys just the same as if it hadn't happened. Wickie was like that. He went crazy sometimes and then got over it right away.

Nat Briggs was a little man with stooped shoulders, but his muscles were as hard as steel. He moved slowly, but with the agility of a cat. He had big grey eyes, and he liked to talk.

When he first came to Scatterfield he got a job with Old John Delaney as a teamster. That didn't last long, because Nat really had a disinclination for steady work. So Old John put him on as odd-job man. He worked by the job and was paid when the job was finished—not before.

Nat said he didn't like to team for Old John, anyway, because he always felt too sorry for the horses. He said the horses were so poor that he always felt ashamed to ride in the wagon. He said he felt like he really ought to get out and help them pull. And that was the way the old man's horses were. They worked more than any other horses in town—on half as much to eat.

The kids had been spending a good deal of time with Nat. He talked to them about faraway places. He brought such places right up to them so that they might see them from his shanty door.

Through Nat's soft voice the gang felt the terrible heat of July in Arizona and they lived through snowbound winters in North Dakota. They lolled about in the lazy springs of Mississippi. They journeyed with Nat around the Cape after he had been shanghaied in San Francisco, and once they spent three months in a convict camp in the Florida swamps. He told the boys about the railroad bulls and how they rapped ice-cold knuckles with a blackjack, injecting pain that would linger for months.

Once Nat gave Soapy a trouncing, and after that Soapy took an uncommon liking to him. It happened because of a cigarette Soapy had rolled for Nat. It was not an ordinary cigarette. It had tobacco in each end and dry horse manure in the middle. Nat gave him a pretty good trouncing then and there, but Soapy didn't let out a peep. In a little bit Nat put his arm about the boy's shoulder and spoke to him.

"Soapy," he said, "you're as ornery as hell, but I reckon ya can't hardly help it. You bin fed on it ever since the day your old lady turned you out. I like ya because ya are ornery. But ya got ta learn ta save your ornery tricks fer guys that deserves them. Git me, Kid?"

"Sure, Nat," Soapy answered. "I gitcha."

After that Nat and Soapy were fast friends.

When the kids got to the shanty that day, they found Nat standing in the doorway, gazing ruefully out through the rain. He was leaning with his shoulder against the doorframe, smoking a cigarette. He smoked almost constantly. Soapy spoke to Nat as they approached the door.

"What're ya doin', Nat?" he asked.

Mark could feel the warm glow from Nat's fire coming out the shanty door. It felt comfortable.

"I'm waitin' fer it ta quit rainin'," Nat answered. "By God, d'ya know there hain't no weather in the world so damned annoyin' as Ohio weather? I tell ya I believe that."

"Oh, it ain't so bad," Soapy ventured.

"How the hell do you know, Soapy?" Nat grinned. "You hain't never bin no place but Scat-

terfield. I tell ya, boy, the winters here are bad.
Cold one day an' warm the next. Freeze an' thaw.
Rain an' snow. It gits a guy's nerves. I hain't goin'
ta stay here another winter if I kin help it. I kin
tell ya that!"

The kids followed Nat into the shanty and sat
down on the cot. Nat straddled a pine box where
he could still look out the shanty door. Nat kept
the door part way open, even in cold weather. The
stove kept the little room too warm. Now little
rivulets of water dropped ceaselessly before the
doorway from atop the low, slanting roof.

"Where ya goin', Nat?" Mark inquired.

"I don't know. . . . Don't know," he answered
slowly. "It's gittin' pretty damned late ta think of
goin' anywhere much."

"What're ya waitin' fer, Nat?" Soapy asked.

"I'm waitin' fer nine dollars and twenty cents."

"Huh?" Soapy asked.

"Nine dollars and twenty cents," Nat repeated.
"The Old Man owes it to me and he won't pay me
'til I'm through with this job of post holes. I bin
waitin' a week ta finish 'em, but it hain't stopped
rainin' long enough ta git anything done.

"I only got six more ta dig. Christ! I'm out of
eats, even, an' if I ask Old John fer tick at the store,
he'll charge me fer three times as much as I buy.
He always does that.

Nat looked forlornly at a lonely can of beans on a shelf above his head and continued.

"There's my supper and my breakfast," he explained. "After them's gone I'll have ta scratch."

Wickie stretched his big mouth and giggled. Nat looked at him and grinned.

"You damned little ape, I don't think ya know when you're hungry," Nat said.

Wickie giggled again. Nat couldn't offend Wickie. Wickie liked him.

"Reverend Hard said that God is responsible fer everythin'," Soapy ventured. "Even the weather. He said that God worked mysterous like. I heard 'im tell that t'Old Man Knowles. D'ya believe that, Nat?"

Nat rolled a cigarette between thin, nervous fingers that were stained yellow. He licked the paper slowly, carefully. Then he stuck a long splinter of wood into the fire, lit the cigarette, and inhaled deeply. He blew a great cloud of blue smoke toward the shanty roof. In three long breaths he exhaled the smoke that lingered in his lungs. It poured from his nostrils in thin, blue streams. His twisted lips moved in a half-smile.

"I don't know, Soapy," he finally answered.

"D'ya believe in God, Nat?" Soapy asked.

Nat got up from his box and stood in the doorway. He stretched his arms above his head and yawned. His grey eyes looked out through the dusk. He looked far beyond John Delaney's lumberyard, into other days and other lands.

"My old man says there hain't none," Soapy ventured anxiously, waiting for an answer.

"I don't know a damned thing about it," Nat answered after a long silence. "It's bin rainin' fer a week. I know that. An' on accounta the rain, I'm out of supplies. Maybe there is a God, and maybe He caused it ta rain. But if there is one, He oughtn't t'have no difficulty in seein' that I'm half starved an' damn near naked!"

The next day was Saturday, and Soapy and Mark had planned to go down to Yellow Creek.

When Mark got up it had stopped raining, but the sky was still covered with a grey blanket. It was an even grey, and he couldn't see a spot of blue anywhere.

After he had fed the stock and milked he went up to Soapy's. He walked in the back kitchen door without knocking. It was about as unclean a place as you could imagine, but Mark liked it. He liked it because he could be as careless as he wanted to be. He could swear with all his might and no one cared. He could take many more liberties there than he could in his own home. That Michael Cullen would have lectured for six months had he ever heard Mark talk in Soapy's house. That boy had certainly learned how to make the air blue with a string of oaths. Mark felt pretty big and important in Soapy's home.

Soapy's mother never swept the floor, to say nothing of a mop, which was sorely needed. Just now the table was full of unwashed breakfast dishes, and a big, green fly, brought to life by the kitchen fire, buzzed about the table. It was the last of its tribe.

Soapy had just got up and was eating a breakfast of greasy fried potatoes. In his right hand he clutched a mug of black coffee, with which he washed them down his throat. His mother sat across the table from him, drinking a glass of hard cider. She had had her breakfast hours before with Old Man Pendleton. The old man had started to the city with a load of junk before daylight. He wouldn't be back until late evening.

Soapy's old mother was a Swede, and she had stringy blonde hair and pale, watery blue eyes. She had a large muscular frame, but one leg was shorter than the other. When she hobbled about the kitchen the bottom of her tattered old dress swished back and forth with rhythmical regularity.

When Mark came in Soapy gulped down what remained of his coffee and got up quickly. The old woman swallowed the rest of her cider. She got up and fished about in the pocket of her dirty checkered apron. She drew forth a box of snuff and with big, calloused thumb and forefinger, stuffed a wad of it into each of her nostrils.

"I'll take the old man's rifle," Soapy said. "Maybe we kin knock over a squirrel fer dinner."

"Old man vale you, boy," the old woman said.

Soapy reached up in the cupboard and got a box of cartridges. He grabbed the rifle from the corner and together he and Mark started out the door.

"Not unless you tell 'im," Soapy said.

"Ol' man vale you," she repeated with lugubrious finality.

"I don't give a damn!" Soapy yelled. "G'by, Old Lady—g'by!"

He knew he would get a beating. He didn't care —because he probably would get one anyway.

Neither Nutsie Doane nor Cockie Werner could go with them. Their old men were home, and they couldn't get away. Wickie went, though. Nothing ever detained Wickie. When Soapy and Mark walked back of where he lived, he ran out and followed them. Mark could see the thin form of his old mother through the back window, as she bobbed up and down over a washtub.

"Got yer rifle, hain't ya, Soapy?" he slobbered gleefully. "I'm goin', too. I'm goin', too!"

The three kids crossed the railroad tracks on Perry Street, and went through an alley that bordered Old John's lumberyard. In an open field back of Nat Briggs' shanty they could see Nat at work digging post holes. He worked furiously, fearing it might rain before he got through. They yelled at him, and he stopped for a moment and waved.

They had very little success that day. They waded about in the mud bottoms along Yellow Creek, but nothing eventful happened. At noon, when they got hungry, they rustled about for something to eat, but they couldn't find anything. All the farmers in the neighborhood had their chickens locked securely in hen houses, away from the weather. They couldn't fish, because the water was high and roily. Mark's stomach got pretty empty, and his head ached like it always did when he got in that famished condition.

Finally they put up a target on a tree and amused themselves by shooting at it. Soapy was a good shot and hit the bull's eye every time, but Mark was only fair. Mark always got nervous when Wickie had the gun. Wickie always jiggled about, and you couldn't tell which direction he would finally shoot.

Kids can't have fun, though, on empty stomachs. Shooting at a mark got tiresome in a short time. They started back about midafternoon.

The air was chill and damp. It was that kind of chill that gets under your clothing and grips your bare body. When the kids got to Kilner's Woods they found a few bits of dry wood and started a fire. The fire was only satisfactory because it warmed them a bit. The wet wood they piled on it generated smoke and made their eyes smart.

They sat around a long while, not saying anything at all. They were too tired and dejected to talk. Mark was thinking about getting home to a warm supper, and wondering why he ever had made such a trip.

In a little while Soapy picked up the rifle and went out among the trees. Mark heard the rifle crack several times but didn't pay any attention. He supposed Soapy was just shooting at an old tin can or a mark of some sort. But when he came back he held a big, fat, red squirrel by its bushy tail. He had caught it right through the eye.

Wickie started to slobber and breathe hard when he saw the blood dripping from the dead squirrel. He always did that when he saw blood. He seemed to like blood. Mark got out a jackknife to skin the squirrel.

"Gee," he said, "now we kin have something to eat!"

"Aw!" Soapy said. "Let's save it fer Nat. Nat hain't had nothin' good to eat fer a long time. You ain't hungry, are ya?"

"Oh, no!" Mark said. "I hain't hungry!"

But Mark could see that Soapy wanted to save the squirrel for Nat, and he said no more. After all, it was Soapy's rifle—and Soapy's squirrel.

They put the fire out in the usual manner, standing around it with the steam rolling about their loins.

"It's a good thing we saved enough ta put it out," Soapy grinned.

"Yeah," Mark answered.

Then they started again toward home. When they reached Nat's shanty, they found it closed and locked. Soapy was disturbed, because he was determined to give the squirrel to Nat. The kids looked all through the lumberyard and peered into Old Delaney's grocery store. The field back of the shanty was enclosed with a new barbed-wire fence.

They were obliged finally to give up the search, and they walked on to the railroad. A big engine stood above Perry Street, taking water from a smoke-blackened tank. It was hooked to a long train of heavily loaded cars. Trains always fascinated the gang, and the three boys stood there, waiting for it to start. A man stood atop the coal tender, holding the water spout. The engine was headed south.

It sighed heavily, while water poured into its gullet. The man stopped the water and fastened the spout into place. The engine whistled shrilly, and began to snort and cough. The wheels turned slowly, and then suddenly churned with lightning speed as they slid over the slippery rail. Smoke shot skyward from the stack with a series of loud reports, like a dozen cannons shot in rapid succession. The wheels gripped the rail again and slowed down. The engine was gaining momentum evenly when it thundered past them.

The air was damp, and a thick blanket of fog had gathered. Darkness was closing in ahead of schedule. And as Mark looked toward the water tank he saw that it was half lost in the mist. While he was looking that way the figure of a man glided swiftly from behind it. He leaped, catlike, for the grab-irons of a hopper. He drew himself deftly into the back shelter. He looked like a phantom.

"It's Nat!" Soapy gasped.

When the car swept past them, Nat waved. Soapy's mouth was open in a gesture of disbelief.

Other cars went swiftly by with noisy clatter. Some of the wheels screamed for oil. When the big, red caboose rolled by, Mark saw a man on the back platform, hanging up a red lantern. The train drew farther and farther into the gloom. Presently they could see nothing of it except the red light that gleamed dimly in the distance.

The faint clicking of wheel and rail joint reached their ears. Soapy stood in the middle of the track gazing after it. The crumpled beak of his battered old cap lay across his left ear, and his uncut blond hair swished about his eyes. Under his left arm, barrel down, he held the rifle. In his right hand the forgotten squirrel dangled helplessly.

"Jesus! I wisht I was goin'!" he said.

Winter dragged slowly, for important events were in the offing. The winter term was to mark the end of grade school for all members of the Scatterfield gang. The kids talked of nothing else. They looked toward freedom. All save only Mark Cullen and Soapy Pendleton would find jobs in the city. Soapy said he would never go to school again—adding that he didn't want to work, either. He said he was going to leave old Dick Pendleton's shack, though.

"I hate him," Soapy said. "I'm goin' ta leave his goddam place. "I'm goin' ta be a hobo, like Nat Briggs."

Soapy wanted to get away from that suspended sentence to Reform School, too. You could tell it worried him. He spoke of it often, particularly after a petty theft. When the people of Scatterfield got to wagging their heads and saying, "That Soap Dodger again," Soapy would look a little frightened.

"They'll be tryin' ta send me up, I reckon," he would say.

Cockie and Nutsie said they would get jobs. Nutsie was to finish school, too. He was in the eighth grade in parochial school in the city. Wickie would pass, because school officials wanted to be rid of him. But Wickie had no plans. Cockie and Nutsie looked toward manhood—thinking of broods of children and a place in the world of men.

But they thought of such things vaguely. Life would assemble itself for them and fit into the scheme of time.

Mark spent a good portion of his time attempting to devise a means of avoiding high school. Michael had the matter well planned. Michael intended to make his departure from schoolwork when Mark graduated. He said he was going to become a real-estate man and live in the city. Mark would have easy access to a good high school there, Michael observed.

Michael dreamed often of the easy money to be made at real estate. (Michael, the peasant, going to live on a paved street with a tiny grass plot behind his house where nothing would grow.) But the man thought of such matters bravely enough.

"I'm goin' ta git a job," Cockie explained proudly.

"An' I already got one promised in the shops where my old man works," Nutsie said. "I'll go ta work when school is out."

And Mark sensed the disintegration of circumstance. He was about to pass through another door, which would close behind him. He would pass on in his own confused and stumbling manner. His life was a series of episodes; each without direction, and each without apparent meaning. They drifted back into the vaults of memory and generated a great sympathy for all things living. It was that sympathy which defeated all his aims and robbed him of hate.

But the events of that last winter in Scatterfield were interrupted. That is, spring was not far away; and the interruption clogged Mark Cullen's brain with darkness into which vague images came to dance with the uneasy rhythm of idiots. Time and reality came to an end. Mark Cullen remained in that dark abyss for many weeks. He took up the threads of life slowly, and climbed again into the world of living creatures.

The thing came upon him with startling suddenness. At midafternoon, dots raced before his eyes, and the sullen print in his geography swam into long, black lines. He straightened up, squinted his eyes, and attempted to bring the black lines into words with meaning. The effort made him dizzy. Into his ears came a wild roaring. The sound rolled into his ears and out again.

He could never remember much of it. Walking home after school, the Delaney Avenue hill appeared before his fever-laden eyes like a mountain. His legs were like lead, and he staggered drunkenly. He climbed and climbed for hours. His breath came in laboring gasps. He wanted to lie down and rest, but a driving impulse sent him staggering on up the mountainside. It was an interminable and endless path. Houses along the path were swollen, and they had pouched sides. Sick . . . sick. . . .

He fixed Judy with his eyes only a moment. He saw her leap, frightened, from her chair. But her figure became immediately indistinct. His books dropped from his hand and banged to the kitchen floor. The words of his mother were driven off in a crazy dance to lose themselves in darkness.

"Why, Mark . . . what's the matter. . . ?"

Her words rolled about his head, rocked into his ears, swam out into nothingness, and came back again. " . . . I heard her twice . . . twice . . . twice . . . twice . . . twice . . . twice. . . . "

The blackness came again, and the roaring noise swept into his ears. It was like wind rolling through black caverns deep in the earth. Words came to him feebly or not at all. There were broken sentences and single words nipping his brain like needles. They were crowded with sick dizziness. He saw Dr. Clarke for only a moment. The physician's face looked bloated, and it sat atop a spindly body. Mark heard his voice.

" . . . typhoid. . . . "

Into the darkness that hung over Mark Cullen for weeks came only dreams. He could give them no sense of time or place. And always he was alone. He remembered them with horror, for they were filled with endless struggle and weary defeat. He

wanted to cease the struggle—to escape the weari-
ness; but he could not.

Once he swam through black, swirling water
that rolled toward him in gigantic waves. He swam
against the waves, and they beat him back. He
pulled with him a heavy weight, tied to his foot.
The weight dragged him back and under the black
water, and he struggled, tired and alone, to the
surface and tried again. He did not call out, for
he knew he was the only person alive in that lonely
world.

And again he wandered alone through a flat monotonous country, barren of all life. Heavy clouds
rolled always overhead, and as he stumbled on he
searched for something; he knew not what. When
the picture vanished he found himself strapped to
the earth, looking over an interminable area filled
with wiry, half-rusted tufts of grass. Snakes glided
in and out of the grass and crawled over his naked
and imprisoned body.

He struggled up a sheer, high cliff, whose rocks
were loosened. And as his bleeding hands clutched
them, they pulled away. For hours he struggled
upward toward the tall trees above him. When he
reached the crest to clutch the vines above his head,
they ripped loose from the soft soil, plunging him
back into darkness. Again and again he struggled
upward toward the vine-covered summit, saying
always, "The vines will pull loose . . . the vines will

pull loose ... the vines will pull loose. ... " The words hammered his ears like the hollow thumping of a drum.

As Mark lay through the weeks, his thin frame melted away. The skin clung tightly to his skull, so that each, ridgelike bone could be easily traced. He lay with open mouth, exposing patches of ulcers inside. His teeth came to look like tusks hanging from skin-covered bone. From deep in hollow sockets, his burning eyes stared straight above him. His arms and legs were strips of tendon and bone.

"If we can break his fever tonight, he may live," said Dr. Clarke. After weeks. ...

A great, agonized sob rolled out of Michael. Stooped, his arms hanging helplessly at his sides, he looked dumbly at the wasted figure of his boy. His jaw dropped, and he shuddered.

Dusk was falling out of doors, and Michael walked slowly ... slowly. He closed the barn door carefully behind him and stood for a moment, staring into the gloom. Then he dropped to his knees. He did not know how to say what he wanted to say.

"God," he mumbled, "O, God, he is all I have. ... O, God, my life has not been easy. ... I want him. ... O, God Almighty. ... I want him to live. ... "

Michael fell forward in the straw, and the sobs that struggled through his throat came forth in agony. They sounded like the spasms of pain in the wild laughter of an idiot. The cow, munching hay, turned her head and fixed her big, round eyes on the huddled figure of Michael. She turned again to the hay. The horse stomped, swished his tail—and rats in the haymow above squealed and thumped their tails upon the floor.

Mark Cullen had to learn to walk again. When he had gathered sufficient strength, Judy helped him out of bed, and he stood for a moment on thin, trembling legs. Then his bony knees buckled. Judy caught him, and he sat down on the bed. Sweat coursed over his thin face.

"I can't make it, Mom," he pleaded. "I can't walk no more."

"Yes, you can, son," said Judy. "Let's try it again."

With Judy's arm supporting him, he tried again. He moved his legs in feeble steps forward, and Judy half-carried him to the middle of the room and back to his bed again. There he lay, exhausted, and a dreamless sleep immediately closed down his eyelids.

For three more weeks Mark remained at home. He felt free, remembering that the other kids were held by four walls of the schoolroom. He sat on the front porch, watching their dull footsteps and remembering that he did not need to go. He took long walks alone. Sometimes he stood for hours, watching John Delaney's men hammer houses together, or he sat, contented, on a rock and watched the water in the brook tumble on its way to Yellow Creek. The spring sun was warming the earth. It would soon be summer.

He was conscious, now, that other gangs of younger boys were banding together. He watched them after school, bound together by some bond of common sympathy, heading for Yellow Creek.

"My gang will soon be broken up," he thought. "The new gangs will do the same as we did, and it won't be much different."

For kids who got out of school to work in shops no longer concerned themselves with racing over the mud bottoms along Yellow Creek. They took their places in the world of men. And Mark, himself, was anxious to be through with school, so that he might reach upward toward manhood. All this thinking brought Mark to the realization that he had missed a lot of school. He started to study at home in an effort to make up the work. He certainly didn't want to fail and have to take his eighth-grade work again. It sickened him to think of it.

Before Mark went back to school, he learned that Soap Dodger Pendleton had been arrested again. Soapy had needed some scrap tobacco, and had gone into John Delaney's grocery store for it. He went in at night through the back window, just as he had often done. Soapy took a pair of cotton pants, too. That was his undoing. Marshal Fogarty had found the pants in the woodshed off Soapy's kitchen door. But Marshal Fogarty did not find the tobacco.

Mark thought there would be no escape for Soapy this time. And he felt sorry about it all. Soapy was his best friend—the best he had ever had. J. Wellingsford Knowles would see to it that Soapy got sent to Reform School this time. When the lad was arrested old Knowles was pleased. Old John Delaney didn't say anything. But Knowles did. Knowles said the Reform School was the only place for such a mean kid.

"You're going where you belong," he told Soapy. "And I hope it will be a lesson to you."

So they took Soapy to the Juvenile Detention Home in the city. There would be a hearing before the judge in a few days, and then everyone expected Soapy to be taken away. Just at about the time when schooldays were over, too. Mark felt pretty badly about it all.

Even Michael said there was no hope of getting Soapy out of trouble this time.

"It's too bad," Michael said, "but maybe it's the only thing to do. Maybe it's the only way to re-form the boy."

No one really cared very much. It was just something to make conversation. And the people of Scatterfield had the matter well thought out. They considered Soapy already in the Reform School—only they didn't know Soapy.

Mark was in his room, and it was dark outside. He lit his lamp, raised the window, and sniffed at the clean air. Then he sat down on his bed and got to thinking about Soapy. He had been sitting there staring at the floor only a few minutes when he heard a loud thump on the floor by the window. The moment he saw the large rock with a note tied around it, he knew that Soapy was out there in the darkness. He leaped up and read it. He held it close to his oil lamp, and his squinting eyes pursued the scrawled lines.

"I busted out of the home," it said, *"and I am down here. Can you come out over the porch."* Soapy.

Mark puffed out the light and put on his jacket. He climbed out the window and to the ground. He heard Soapy whistle, and then he saw him creep out of the shadows back of the house. He looked natural enough to Mark, as he crept into the ray of light coming from the window. His cheek was bulging with a chew of tobacco, and his face was dirty. His uncut hair swished about his eyes. He had on a pair of long pants much too large for him, and they were tied about his middle with a rope. He carried a package.

"Fer Christ's sake, Mark," Soapy whispered, "let's git out of here. They're a-lookin' fer me everywhere."

He started to run, and Mark followed. They took to the alley, and after they got safely into darkness, dropped into a walk.

"I busted out of the joint this morning," Soapy explained. "They set me to washin' windows, and I jist run fer it. When I got out of town, I cut through fields and stayed clean away from roads. Jesus, I betcha I walked ten miles.

"Well, sir, I come up the alley back of your house and snuk into the barn. I hid there 'til dark in yer old man's haymow. Why I was a-hidin' there when yer old man tossed hay down to the hoss. He damn near stuck me with the fork."

"What are ya goin' do?" Mark asked.

"They's a freight a-settin' at the crossin', and I'm gonna grab it," Soapy said.

"What ya got in the package?"

"That there is the terbaccer I stold from Old John."

The boys moved like shadows into Old John's lumberyard, crossed the road, and slipped up behind the water tank at the railroad. The big engine puffed anxiously and sobbed. Its fiery eye pierced the darkness far down the track. A man atop the coal tender fastened the water spout and climbed into the cab. In the black darkness at the end of

the train, a lantern completed a half-circle signal
and disappeared. The engine whistled, snorted, and
moved. Soapy turned to Mark.

"I wanted to see you a-fore I went," he said.
"And I wanted to git my terbaccer. I had it hid
down the brook."

The cars rattled and rolled. Cinders dropped
through the darkness like hail. Soapy moved toward the train and stopped a moment.

"So long, Mark," he hollered. "You been a good
feller."

Then Soapy darted out into the darkness like a
cat. He swung himself aboard a gondola with the
ease of Nat Briggs. Mark thought of Nat Briggs.
And the train rolled on toward the faraway horizon. It lost itself in darkness.

> *So long, Soapy. The narrow rules men
> built their lives upon were not for you.
> Your short life was a poem, and there was
> no need to express it. Stand in empties. Ride
> the rattlers. And let the world rush past
> you. Let them build their cities and grow
> heavy with the fatness of success. Grimy
> men carry dinner pails, and their lean wom-
> en heave yammering kids into the world.
> But you swing toward far horizons, while
> the low-flying smoke from the engine
> smears you with all the marks of the road.*
> *Watch heavy waves roll over the wide
> Dakota wheat fields. Listen to the mourn-*

*ful whistle of chugging steamboats on the
Mississippi, and watch belching steel mills
in Pittsburgh spew their crimson glare across
the darkened sky. Ride a fast rambler to
the coast and watch fog roll in through the
Golden Gate to imprison ships in San Francisco Bay. Carve your initials on black
water tanks, and listen to the jargon of 'bos
and bindlestiffs in jungle camps by the
roadside.*

*Button your coat around the brake rod,
Soapy, when sleep invades your smarting
eyes and cinders cut your face like needles.
Listen to the whistle of the engine boring
the darkness far ahead. Do you hear the
whining wheels as they click over the rail
joints?*

*Roll on through the sun-baked desert,
Soapy, and clatter over green fields in Illinois. When sullen skies spit snow in the
autumn, head for Mississippi—and keep a
sharp eye out for the railroad bulls. She's
a-rollin', Soapy. Don't miss that rusty grab
iron. Pull yourself up, and stand for a moment on the drawbars and watch the ties
race beneath your feet.*

*So long, Soapy. . . . You are separate and
apart. Clatter over an endless and dizzy
world. Another junction lies just ahead . . .
always and forever there are junctions in
the distance. So long, Soapy. . . . So long. . . .*

Michael wanted to be a companion to his boy,
and he realized that he was not. Sometimes he made

an awkward effort to get back of that wall of silence that had grown between them. Michael knew it was there, but his bungling effort to tear it down always ended in failure. Both boy and man misunderstood each other. Mark always felt timid in the presence of his father, and when they talked together, he was embarrassed. Strangely enough, Michael fought the same emotion. But Michael fought it with sarcasm directed at his son.

Years later, when Michael sat in a lonely corner looking into the mists of long ago, he could make only small talk with his son. Stooped with age and fumbling with thought, he understood that he did not know his son—that they were really strangers. Michael watched the changing patterns of life from the obscurity of age in those later years. It was then he needed the companionship of his son. But they fumbled about with talk, embarrassed in each other's presence. It was too late.

In that last swift-moving spring in Scatterfield, Michael had high hopes for his boy. There were great things in the future, and he expected to shape destiny to his will. In his mind he had shaped a career for Mark, which the boy would certainly follow. All of which brought Michael the conviction that he must talk with the boy. The thought pleased him. A father, he thought, ought to be a companion to his children.

Mark followed his father into the shadowy room

that night, and sat down by the window. A light from the kitchen where Judy was preparing supper tossed itself through the doorway. At the time, Michael's manner was kindly, and his gestures appeared sympathetic. He sat in an easy chair and began to rub his finger over his nose thoughtfully.

Sitting in a straight chair by the window, Mark was glad that his father had not bothered to light a lamp. He was embarrassed, and felt like a stranger before Michael. Michael cleared his throat.

"Have you been a pretty good boy lately?" he asked. His voice was kindly. Mark's embarrassment deepened, and the palms of his hands went to sweating. He rubbed them over his pants.

"Why, I guess so," he faltered.

> *Michael, your boy was old enough at that time to have a wider knowledge than a small child. He was old enough to be visited by dark desire. He had learned many things in the gutters of Scatterfield. Perhaps, that night, you might have torn away the wall between you and your son. And the boy would have worshipped you throughout all his days. For he needed you, then, Michael.*

Michael stumbled on.

"Well, son," he said. "I want you always to be a good boy."

Michael had thought out all that he wanted to say to Mark, but was finding it difficult. He was having a struggle with that friendly little talk. He cleared his throat auspiciously.

"We're going to get into the city after you graduate," he said, "so that you'll have access to a good high school."

Mark said nothing. He continued to rub the palms of his damp hands over his pants and look from the window into the gloom. He heard a railroad whistle and thought how lucky Soapy was.

"A good high school will prepare you for college," Michael continued. "Have you given any thought to what you want to take in college, son?"

"No."

Michael, a little irritated, rubbed his hands together and leaned forward.

"That's the trouble with you, son," he said. And still his voice did not betray his irritation. "I'm afraid you don't give much thought to anything."

Mark said nothing.

"Well," Michael continued, "I have thought the whole matter out for you. I want to make a lawyer out of you. Let's see—you'll have four more years in high school. Then you can take a two-year arts course and follow it with four years of law. You'll still be a youngster when you finish. You will get a good start in life."

Michael, did you understand that ten years seemed an eternity to the boy? Did you understand how his mind revolted under dullness?

"I don't want to be no lawyer," Mark said finally. He spoke in such a low voice that Michael scarcely heard him.

"Well, what the devil do you want to be?" he hollered. "You've got to be something. Do you want to be a ditchdigger, like the rest of the infernal riffraff around this town? You'll never be strong enough for manual labor. You've got to get an education."

Mark did not answer. He sat silently, looking from the window into the darkness. He saw nothing but darkness.

Michael now imitated a simpleton. His inference, thinly veiled, was aimed at Mark.

"Well," he said, affecting the tone of a fool, "what do you want to be, a cleaner of backhouses?"

"No."

"What do you want to be?" he said angrily.

"I don't wanna be anything that you have to go to school for. I wanna quit school."

Michael, thoroughly angry, leaped from his chair and stood glaring down at Mark.

"Well, you're going on to school, I can tell you that!" he hollered. "I'll see that you do. You've got to do as I say. You're a minor child. Do you understand?"

Mark drew his head into his shoulders and said nothing.

"Do you understand?" Michael bellowed again.

He stepped close to the boy. "You little simpleton."

"I understand what you said," Mark said. His words came from his throat in almost a whisper. Michael stepped back, certain now, that he had imposed his will upon the boy.

"All right, then," he said. "Let's have no more of that kind of talk."

Michael and Mark did not speak throughout the remainder of the evening. Long after Michael had fallen into slumber that night, Mark crept forth from his own bed. Down the darkened stairway he crept, to rummage about in Michael's desk. When he returned to his room he carried with him a long, printed slip labeled "Eighth Grade Examinations." And they contained all that Mark must know to be graduated from grade school. He shared his pilfered knowledge with Cockie Werner and Wickie Winters.

Late in May that year, Mark was graduated. His grades were excellent, as were those of Cockie Werner and Wickie Winters. Wickie's grades were surprising to school officials who did not know how patiently Mark and Cockie had worked with Wickie, teaching him all the answers.

Graduation exercises didn't amount to much. Margaret Castell played "Put On Your Old Gray Bonnet" on the rattly old piano, and Old Man Light gave a little talk. He thanked everyone in

Scatterfield for "co-operating" with him. He said that the class was about to "go out and face the world," adding that he thought they were well prepared for it.

While the Reverend Hard gave the benediction, Mark got to thinking about that time long ago when the preacher stopped Soapy and asked him what his name was.

"What might your name be, little man?" old Hard had said in about as kindly a tone as you could imagine.

"It might be Jesus Christ, but it hain't," Soapy answered him. Then Soapy spit tobacco juice and darted away, leaving the amazed minister staring after him. But that was a long time before and the Reverend Hard hadn't been in Scatterfield very long. He soon learned about Soapy. Now Mark sat in the schoolroom, listening to the minister and wishing that Soapy were there so that they might have a little fun. Michael passed out the diplomas, and the kids walked out of the battered old school for the last time—and none of them were sorry.

Mark walked up Delaney Avenue alone, looking out over Scatterfield's barren hills bleaching in the bright sunshine and remembering that tomorrow he was to move away from the town and never be a part of it again. He saw Limpy Peters pump himself into his drugstore far over on Perry Street, and at the top of the hill beyond the ravine, he saw

the lean form of Charlie Heston. Charlie was
planting seed in his garden. In the distance he
heard the clatter of hammers, as Old John Delaney's
men banged another house together. Everything
seemed pretty familiar to the boy.

At the Delaney Avenue bridge, he saw Mary
Hartman standing alone. A little embarrassed, he
walked on toward her, and she watched him.

"Hi, Mary," he said.

The dreary picture of that winter day when he
coasted over the Delaney Avenue hill with Mary
still clung to his mind. But he no longer resented
the little girl. He just didn't think much about
her. Just the same he observed that her little breasts
were beginning to swell beneath her clean gingham
apron. Her hips were rounding into curved lines,
too. Mary Hartman was a pretty girl.

"If you'll wait a minute," she said as he walked
past her, "I'll walk up the hill with ya, Mark."

Mark walked slowly until she was abreast of him.

"You're gonna move, hain't ya, Mark?" she
ventured.

"Yeah," Mark said indifferently.

"I wisht ya wasn't," she said. And her voice was
strange. She placed her hand on his arm. Mark
looked about apprehensively, but the bedraggled
folk walking up the hill didn't seem to notice. He
looked at the little hand on his arm. It was white
as marble, and little blue veins coursed their way

beneath the skin. Desire crept through him, and he was ashamed.

"Yeah," he said. "I do, too."

"Mark," she said.

"Yeah."

"I still like you a awful lot, Mark. Even if you don't like me no more."

She spoke simply, and her lips trembled. His desire for her was half pity.

"I do like ya, Mary," he insisted. But his words were lies. He neither liked nor disliked her. His feeling was one of desire and shame. He wanted to put his arm about her, but not in a gesture of comfort. He thought only of his hand, gliding over her little rounded breasts. The impulse deserted him as he stood before the front gate of his Scatterfield home. Mary looked up at him. Her eyes were as blue as the sky overhead.

"G'bye, Mary," he said.

"Mark," she faltered. "Mark—d'ya really like me?"

"Yeah. I like ya, Mary."

"G'bye, Mark," she said. And then she walked on up the street, leaving Mark standing alone, and feeling pretty important. Mary Hartman walked straight on without looking back. She walked out of Mark Cullen's life, and he never saw her again.

Two horse-drawn moving vans pulled up to the

Cullens' door early next morning, to haul the furniture out of that yellow town. Michael's horse and cow went to Old Dick Pendleton. Old Dick gave Michael a note for the animals, and never paid it.

Michael and Judy and Mark walked out over the cinder path along Delaney Avenue together. The sun was warm, and swarms of kids trooped toward the hills in the distance and to Yellow Creek beyond. School was out, now, and only lazy days lay ahead for the new gangs of kids banding together in Scatterfield.

The same tattered awning flapped in the breeze before John Delaney's grocery store. A skinny woman with a lean, sallow face, walked into the door. She carried a market basket. A group of kids moved silently, apprehensively back of a pile of lumber in the lumberyard. Latherup Jones stood before the door of his barber shop, chewing a stogie and watching the Cullens with doleful eyes. And Flossie Kershner sat silently before her doorway.

Judy Cullen looked from the window of the old and battered streetcar. She looked toward yellow hills, strewn with hovels and shacks. A bearded man walked into an outhouse across the street, and an old grocery wagon with flapping side curtains lost itself in clouds of dust in the distance. The car jerked and moved.

It picked up speed. It leaped and bounded and jumped in a noisy exploration of the uncertain

rails between Scatterfield and the city. Scatterfield danced madly back into memory.

"I'm glad we're getting out of this wretched
hole," said Judy Cullen.

3

IF YOU chance to visit that section of an Ohio town known as Scatterfield, you will doubtless be startled by a grotesque granite memorial to a soldier. Atop the great slab, which stands at the junction of Delaney Avenue and Clara Street, is the statue of an American Doughboy.

The slab itself is so large that the soldier appears small and feeble. In his left hand he holds a hand grenade and in the right, an army rifle. His mouth is open as though he were about to shout, but his features fail to reveal a fierce and fighting spirit. Somehow the sculptor fastened a look of fear on the soldier's face.

The slab bears this inscription:

PENDLETON'S POINT

The junction of these two streets shall
hereafter be known as Pendleton's
Point in memory of

OLIN PENDLETON

Who was the first American soldier from
Scatterfield to lose his life in France.
He died at Chateau-Thierry, June 3,
1918, in defense of his country.
This memorial was raised by popular
subscription, under direction of

JOHN DELANEY
March 4, 1925

The clay remnants of the body of Soap Dodger
Pendleton are deeply buried in the Scatterfield
graveyard. And over the head of that young lad
there is no marker. The earth has settled, and where
it dropped away more earth has been dumped.
Unless you knew where Soapy was buried you could
not find his grave.

Soap Dodger Pendleton came home to Scatterfield
in a pine box. And Old Dick Pendleton was not
there to greet him as he always did in the old days.
No one knew where Soapy's folks were. The soldier was brought to his native soil only because he
gave Scatterfield as his home when he enlisted.

The President of the United States spoke over
the body of Soapy Pendleton before he was carried
back to his home.

"These poor bodies are but the clay sentiment
once possessed of human souls that flamed in patri-
otic devotion; lighting new hopes on the battle-
grounds of civilization. . . . "

Thus spoke the President; but Soapy's ears were
stopped. He could not hear.

Soapy traveled over the world before he went
to war. He dodged railroad bulls with a skill that
made old hoboes green with envy. And he never
went hungry, for he was an expert thief. He slept
in jails from Maine to California, but authorities
never pinned a job on him.

That dark night in June a whining shell pinned

Soap Dodger Pendleton's body to the ground just the same. Soapy was searching for something. He was hungry. And as he crawled alone over the dark, uneven ground beyond his trench, he heard the shell. It ripped through the night and whined. He heard the bellowing explosion but felt nothing at first.

When he started to crawl on he discovered that his legs would not move. Then he felt warmth creeping over his back. An exploring hand told him that the warmth was blood. It was a struggle for Soapy to get into that shell hole and look up at the stars, but he made it. His blood was spilling fast.

Maybe Soapy figured that his life had just come out even, for there was only one chew of scrap tobacco in his package. He stuffed it into his mouth and chewed and spit and looked into the high dark sky. The sky soon grew black with only occasional waves of light trembling over it. And then Soapy's mouth dropped open and he could not taste the tobacco. He grew too tired to be conscious of the terrible thirst burning his throat. That was just before darkness swallowed all of him.

If you search the newspaper files of a certain Ohio city in 1929, you will find two news stories concerning members of the old Scatterfield gang. They appeared the same day. One story is only two paragraphs in length and states briefly that Henry Doane, of Scatterfield, took his own life by slashing his wrist with broken glass. Doane, who had been an invalid for many years, was despondent over ill-health, you will find.

The second story, an eight-column banner, will inform you that Clarence Winters of Scatterfield attacked his former sweetheart, brutally slashed her throat with a razor, and left her to die in her own blood. You will find, too, that when the sheriff's men arrested Wickie at his home, he reached for a butcher knife.

"Is she dead yet?" the story quotes him as saying. "By God, if she's not, I'll go back an' finish her!"

The trial of Wickie Winters was declared a triumph for speedy justice. It was rushed through to its conclusion, and a solemn judge sentenced Wickie to die in the electric chair.

And during the trial Wickie sat always before the jury. He sat there with his wide mouth open and his simian head drawn close to his bony shoulders. His dull eyes were fastened on the floor. Drool crept frequently from his lips, and his long, red tongue lay idly between his teeth. Sometimes he panted hoarsely.

He was there for the jury to see, but so, too, were the blood-stained garments of the dead girl. Psychiatrists who examined Wickie told the jury that he was sufficiently sane to know and judge his own acts. But neither the psychiatrists nor the jury had ever witnessed Wickie so many years ago as he tore the entrails from living fish, or as he gleefully sawed the head from a rabbit. His gestures at the time were those of sheer pleasure.

The prison chaplain was afraid of Wickie Winters. For Wickie clutched the bars in Death Row and howled. His eyes were wild, and he panted hoarsely. The chaplain stood outside and asked the condemned man if he did not want to pray. Wickie whispered his answer.

"No," he said softly, and he slobbered and gasped. His eyes were flaming with excitement. "No. I don't want to pray. I want to cut your throat an' watch the red blood."

Wickie clenched the bars before his skinny frame until the bony knuckles were white. Then one of his arms dropped clumsily like that of a sick monkey, and he whined. He scooped the froth from his chin with an agile tongue. The chaplain, with wide and unbelieving eyes, raced down the long corridor. The wild screams of Wickie Winters followed him.

"Fer Christ's sakes, take that goddam monkey outa here!" wailed another gaunt fellow who waited for death. But they didn't take him out until he marched toward the steel door at the far end of the long corridor.

So Wickie Winters died without benefit of clergy.

Between two staunch guards he danced on nervous feet toward the sinister door that led into blue and flaming death. His wide lips were inflamed and raw because a long wet tongue continually circled them.

A dozen witnesses saw blue death race through the wasted body of Wickie. They saw the thing before them and nothing more. For their eyes could not penetrate the mists of long ago. They could not see the withered form of Wickie's old mother bobbing up and down over a steaming washtub in Scatterfield while Wickie raced over the mud bottoms along Yellow Creek. Ah, old woman, was it for this you spread your aching loins so many years ago? Was it for this you brought this twisted thing into being?

Nutsie Doane grew tired of lying on his back and looking at his two wasted legs pointing grotesquely toward the ceiling of his dirty room. The legs were thin and useless. They had been paralyzed because the young doctor in Fort Wayne who operated on the lad didn't fully understand nerve centers in the human body.

Nutsie had a good job in Fort Wayne, for he was a skilled mechanic. It was a shame, his family said, to lose a job like that. And it got to be a tedious matter, looking after Nutsie, so his married sister said. He was as helpless as a baby.

Nutsie was such a young lad when he contracted

gonorrhea from that Fort Wayne whore. He didn't know much about the disease, and he didn't treat it at once. He didn't see a doctor until the urinary tract became congested. He had to do something then. He fainted in the hospital, and when he woke up the young physician had split his belly all the way down. Dr. Clarke always said that was a mistake. Nutsie said he didn't know anything about such matters. He only knew that he never would walk again.

And it got tiresome, lying there in his sister's home year after year—exercising his shoulders each morning on the steel bar above his head. For many years Nutsie thought maybe he might recover sufficiently to walk a little. That would have been a help. But finally he gave up.

Nutsie's sister was especially irritable that day. She seemed nervous. Already Nutsie could tell that a kid was coming, for her dress bulged about the abdomen. Nutsie had seen that so often he had grown sick of it.

When his sister brought him his lunch she dropped a glass of water. It spilled over Nutsie's shoulders, and the glass broke when it fell to the floor.

"God damn it!" she yelled. "Every time I come in this God damn room and look at you I break something. You're more damned trouble than you're worth."

Nutsie felt pretty bad about it as he lay alone, thinking hard. He could hear the kids at play outside. They hollered like the old gang used to holler, he reflected. But he had thought of those old days so much that he was tired of that, too. He was tired of everything, and it seemed a waste of time to live as he had to live.

His room was cluttered with all the useless junk that his sister's family didn't want. It was used as a storeroom for forgotten things.

Now, as the afternoon wore on, Nutsie observed a dark storm cloud gathering in the west. He tried to visualize the rain and lightning but his mind revolted. He had seen thousands of storms break over Scatterfield and in his silent room had listened to the crashing violence of thunder—to the rain roaring against his windowpane.

The odor of fried potatoes came up to him from the kitchen—the kitchen he had not seen for many years. His sister would be coming up to his room again shortly, bringing another tray of food— bringing a supply of energy so that his crippled body might remain alive. He was a little sick, thinking about that, too.

Presently his eye caught the bits of broken tumbler his sister had dropped on the floor. Laboriously he shifted his body to the edge of the bed, and he picked up the largest piece. His melancholy eyes examined it. Then, deliberately, he placed the sharp edge of it against his left wrist. The wrist was bent and crooked where years ago it had been broken by a fall at Yellow Creek.

Nutsie pressed hard. He gouged at the tough tendons in the wrist and swept the jagged glass into the artery. He drew it away and looked with horrified eyes, not believing what he saw. Too late. His breath came in sobs, and he sank back on the bed and looked at the ceiling. A crimson fountain spurted from his wrist.

As the storm broke, Nutsie raised his head and and then dropped a little forward over the arm. His useless legs jiggled with effort. Nutsie moaned and then all was silent. The jets of blood leaping from his arm dwindled into a feeble stream and began to clot.

Lightning flashed, and heavy peals of thunder rolled after it. The curtains on Nutsie's open window waved and fluttered, and a mighty torrent of rain rattled on the floor within. It crept swiftly over the floor, climbed over a pile of broken furniture, and splashed against the bed.

Tiny beads of water sprinkled the lifeless fingers of Nutsie Doane. The fingers, still clutching a blood-stained hunk of broken glass, had been yellowed with nicotine. Now the brown of them was green. The curtains flapped, and the rain increased. A fly crawled over Nutsie's bald head. His crooked arm stretched over the edge of the bed. Beneath the

taloned hand was a great pool of crimson blood
slowly seeping into the worn and threadbare carpet.

Only a few Scatterfield folk went to the funeral
of Nutsie Doane. For Nutsie had been dead a long
time, so far as they were concerned. At least he
had been hidden from the world, and the world
had forgotten him.

When L. W. Holt's hearse passed by the poolroom
of Cockie Werner there was no pause. Cockie sat
before the door with a white apron over his heavy
belly. For there was a first-class speakeasy in the
rear of the establishment, and that Cockie tended
bar like an expert.

Cockie watched the hearse roll by and reflected
that maybe he should have gone to Nutsie's funeral.
His lazy mind now conjured many a picture of the
old days. Yeah, he should have gone, he thought.
Nutsie was a hell of a good fellow in his day.

"But, Christ," mumbled Cockie Werner, "I don't
see what good it'd do fer Nutsie."

If you had known Lew Vortz long ago in Scatterfield you wouldn't recognize him now. The
huge muscles in his arms that used to swell and
roll under smooth skin have shriveled away.
Pouches of flabby skin cover what's left of them
in a multitude of puckers, like a loose untailored
garment stitched to his bones. He still wears a blue

work shirt, open at the collar, just as he did long ago, but his thick chest has dropped into a concavity. The rib bones trace themselves through it in a grotesque design. The two points of his breastbone stick out like driven spikes to which the stiff cords in his scrawny neck are fastened. The coarse hair on his chest has turned an ugly grey. The hair on his head is grey and thin. It lies over his forehead in a tangled mat, and the ends of it are twisted and interlocked with his shaggy eyebrows.

His cheeks are drawn in close to his toothless gums and almost always covered with a week's growth of faded whiskers. His beard looks like wiry, half-rusted patches of grass growing in hollow, earthy depressions after the terrific heat of summer has drawn out both color and energy. His eyes are deeply sunk in their sockets and covered with a film. Grey moats encircle them. Sometimes they discharge a torrent of meaningless and absurd tears to course through the wrinkles in his face, where they dry unnoticed.

He lives alone, now, where he lived long ago, in that little house on Delaney Avenue, just across from the Scatterfield graveyard. Scatterfield has changed, too. It is part of the city, now, and Delaney Avenue is paved with brick. A new generation of dirty children play about in the street, but they have no care for Lew. Rather, they fear him a little. They watch him as he goes wheezing and

mumbling about the yard in his bare feet. They
point and whisper and scurry away. But Lew's
face is a dull expression of forgetfulness. He
doesn't care. Sometimes old faces, old ideas, come
tapping on the walls of his mind. But they tap
very gently and with little hope of stirring the
torpid memory lying within.

In summer, Lew works every afternoon in his
garden. The hot sun beats down on his wasted back,
and his blue shirt becomes drenched with sweat.
He hoes tomatoes, potatoes, sweet corn—which
must yield him a supply of food for winter. When
the sun begins to drop toward the horizon he puts
up his hoe and goes panting and wheezing around
to sit on his front steps. His shirt clings to his
withered frame like a wet garment over a human
skeleton. With clumsy, trembling fingers he fills
an old cob pipe with tobacco and clinches the stem
of it far back in his mouth so that the bowl is only
a few inches from his lips. He mumbles to himself
a little, as though he were going through a ritual,
and then lights the pipe. He takes a few eager,
wheezy sucks at it and then sits silently, staring into
the distance. The blue shaft of smoke coming
from the pipe curls feebly, dwindles into a trembling, grey thread and finally dies. Lew forgets to
relight it.

He sits leaning forward, watching the shadows
lengthen slowly. His drool-covered lips make little

noises like a fish breathing close to the water's surface. After a time the drool from his mouth steals
down the pipestem and gathers at the base of the
bowl. It clings there a while and then drops to his
knee, mingling with the sweat of his body. The
shadows creep silently across the street and into the
weed-ridden graveyard; laying cool black hands on
the rotting old headstones and implements of labor
which mark the clay sleeping garments of tired
workers. The afternoon sun drops a damp, spongy
hand over shadow and graveyard alike.

Things begin to look vague in the dusk. He can
scarcely make out the outline of the new four-room
brick schoolhouse far on the hill beyond the graveyard. But the schoolhouse doesn't mean anything
to Lew anyway. It stands where Charlie Heston's
shanty used to be. The shanty ought to be there
yet; and about now Charlie's frail, old wife would
be cooking supper on a coal stove. Smoke would be
rolling comfortably out of a crooked tin chimney.
But if that were true, Lew would be a strong man
sitting in his kitchen. His nimble fingers would be
fumbling restlessly at the pages of a book written
by Karl Marx. His black eyes would be drinking
in the words eagerly. His old mother would be
rocking little Danny to sleep and singing German
lullabies. But the shanty is not there. Only a red
brick schoolhouse which looks clean and stiff and
new. Old Charlie and his wife are just across the

road; their bodies wrapped in soggy clay. And his little boy, Danny, and his old mother, they are across there, too. There are two great boulders marking the place. Crude and uneven letters have been chiseled in them. One of them reads: DANNY VORTZ 1907-1913. The other: MOTHER: DIED 1914. Lew wheeled the boulders there himself from Yellow Creek, long ago, and chiseled the words in them.

Let's see, how old would Danny be now? What year is this? Anyway, he would be a man.

Old wells of suffering and grief have been sealed up in Lew's brain for a long time. Everything is old and long ago. The old man's fancy idles over them almost pleasantly.

But the chill fingers of night are clutching at Lew's withered frame. With bony fingers he removes the pipe from his mouth and gets unsteadily to his feet. He clasps his shrunken chest and coughs feebly. He opens his mouth, exposing the red, shriveled gums within and coughs again and yet again. His trembling jaws chew at the phlegm he has brought forth from deep in his throat. He bends forward and allows it to run from his lips in a thick, sticky stream. His efforts leave him exhausted, and he stands for a moment, wheezing and panting, and looks out into the darkness. Then he walks slowly around the house and into the kitchen door.

Lew's kitchen is just like it used to be. There is

the same table, scarred and battered, and there is no covering on the floor. The pine boards are full of long needlelike splinters. Most everyone in Scatterfield now has gas and electric lights, but in Lew's kitchen there is the same coal range and oil lamp. Now, he lights the lamp and begins preparing his supper. He lifts his ancient bare feet carefully, fearing the splinters, and they come down in dull, unsteady thuds to the floor. He first slices a ripe tomato and then cuts several hunks of stale bread from a partly used loaf.

After this he goes out doors again and into the cellar, where he gets a piece of cheese and a quart bottle of beer. Later he sits slumped in an old battered chair, while the bread and cheese and tomato become an unmasticated wad in his toothless mouth. His quivering old jaws munch at it, and he rolls it over his tongue in a final taste. Then he washes it through his gullet with foamy beer. After he has finished the beer he sits stupidly for a time, mumbling incoherent words. The beer gnaws pleasantly at his stomach, and its soothing heat permeates his bowels.

In a little while Lew goes into his bedroom carrying the lamp. Slowly he withdraws the shirt and trousers from his painful, rheumy body. He swells his shrunken cheeks, puffs out the light, and crawls into bed, drawing the covers over his chest.

The noises of Ohio's summer night come through

the open window to crash and thud against the walls of the room. A multitude of noises. Frogs croak in the ravine beyond the graveyard. Crickets and katydids scream and cry, and a sage old owl hoots a mournful inquiry. There are children in the street before the house playing noisily at go-sheepy-go and blindman's buff. Far away a railroad engine whistles, and the faint rumble of rolling iron wheels comes softly into the room. But under the anaesthesia of age the noises blend and become immediately indistinct, as though they are being gathered up in a giant hand which sweeps them far, far away. Into the old man's brain steals a silence so old that it is forgotten.

. . . As Old Lew potters feebly about his house and garden these days he remembers bits and incidents from years ago. They come back like fragments of half-forgotten dreams. Yesterday though. . . . It is never possible to remember with accuracy what happened yesterday. The cold winter night that Danny died . . . and the funeral. His fumbling brain ponders over this as one might look at a worn and indistinct old painting.

It was bitter cold that night in January, long ago. A blizzard swept howling and shrieking over Scatterfield's hills where hovels and shacks squatted like dark quivering shadows. Rays of feeble, flickering light showed forth from kitchen windows where work-worn people had locked themselves for

warmth and comfort. Windows and loose clap-
boards rattled in ominous protest as the wind
pierced through frail buildings. Smoke from kitch-
en stoves poured forth to hover for a silent moment
above chimney tops, where, caught up in the wild
wind, it danced madly away to dissolution. The
pale moon had climbed up from the east to hurl
itself through black, wind-riven clouds in the sky.
Its mellow light tinged Scatterfield's huge blanket
of snow with yellow.

Little Danny lay on an old couch in Lew's kitchen
that night. He had been sick three days with pneumonia, and Dr. Clarke said he might not live. Lew's
old mother hovered over the boy anxiously, poul-
ticing his chest with onions. The pungent smell of
them permeated the house. Lew stood before the
red-hot stove, thoughtlessly rubbing the heat into
his calloused hands. It was warm in the room, and
there was plenty of coal to spare. The old woman
had waddled far down the railroad track before
dark, gathering it in a sack. She had wrapped a
shawl about her head and another about her shoulders. She heaved the coal to her shoulder like a man
and waddled back. Her fat belly jiggled with each
ungainly step she took.

Lew stood with his back to Danny, because he
couldn't bear to see his frightened, fever-laden eyes
roaming forever around the room. There was a
smudge of dirt across Danny's cheek, and beneath

it his soft skin was crimson with fever. His little mouth hung open as he gasped for breath. On a chair by the couch were several glasses of pink medicine, some pills and spoons.

Lew's feet were clad only in wool socks. His trousers were held in place by suspenders which looped over his broad, muscular shoulders. The sleeves of his blue shirt were rolled to the elbow, and his bared chest was exposed to the hot stove. His brow was raised in a helpless gesture, and he stared silently at the range top. Cold air crept insistently about the windows and stole beneath a wide crack under the door where a strip of frost lay like a silver ribbon. From time to time Lew opened the top of the stove with a lifter and put in more coal. The fire roared and crackled. Lew had waited there, hopelessly.

It was nearly midnight when the scarlet in Danny's cheeks turned to a bleached whiteness. His frightened, choked-up eyes found a single spot in the ceiling at which they bulged and stared. The old woman drew off the onion poultice from Danny's cooling chest. She rolled the boy's body in a blanket and gathered it in her trembling arms. She sat down in a battered old rocking chair and began to rock. *"Ach, mein Gott!"* she wailed, as she placed her withered face against Danny's cheek, where the warmth of recent life was slowly departing. Lew sat down on the couch and drew on his shoes, hooking the laces with clumsy, trembling fingers. He put on his black, threadbare overcoat and went out the back door, slamming it behind him.

When he came back, he brought Mr. Holt, the undertaker, whose fat, pudgy face glowed with sympathy. Lew sat down at the battered old table and signed a note for fifty dollars, payable to L. W. Holt. Then he and the old woman went into the other room.

In return for this consideration, Mr. Holt took the choked look away from Danny's face and washed the dirt smudge off his cheek. He fastened a complacent smile on the boy's lips with glue, and combed his blond hair. When he had finished with his work Danny looked as though he were about to open his eyes and say, "Hie there you! *Wie Gehts!*"

Bit by bit the old man remembers.

On the day of Danny's funeral the weather turned warmer. The sky was cloaked in a heavy grey blanket, and the air was full of blue mist. A cold, drizzling rain seeped through the heavy atmosphere. The snow was slipping away from the face of the steep hill beyond the graveyard, exposing yellow, ulcerous spots of naked earth. Scrub pines bordered the spots like green, gangrenous sores. Charlie Heston's shanty swayed ominously at the crest of the hill like a drunken man about to leap into the valley below. Across the street from Lew's house, Mike and Paddy O'Toole were at work digging Danny's grave—opening a cavernous clay mouth which would soon swallow Danny.

And Lew stood in his front door and watched them, clutching in his hand a mug of untasted beer. The beer had gone flat, and dried foam clung to the sides of the mug. Lew watched until his bedraggled neighbors began to come, mumbling worn and sympathetic phrases.

Lew did not mingle with his neighbors at the graveside. He stood a little back. Awkwardly he stood, clutching his hat in a fist clenched so tightly that the muscles in his forearm knotted and bulged. His jaws were clenched tightly, too, as though he were trying to crush the bone.

Other Scatterfield folk stood about under umbrellas. The old woman, with an apron gathered before her eyes, sobbed and moaned.

Lew stood alone. Drops of rain pierced his face like a thousand needles. His matted hair was soaked, and little globules of water clung to his thick eyebrows. In the offing Mike and Paddy O'Toole stood, leaning on long-handled shovels. The flanks of their breeches were soiled and caked with yellow clay. They spat tobacco juice into pools of muddy water and waited.

The minister, shielding his leather Bible from the rain, began to speak in a smooth, monotonous voice.

At a signal from the fat undertaker, the straps holding Danny's casket sagged, and it began its slow descent into the muddy grave.

"Ashes to ashes. . . . " said the minister smoothly, as he sifted rose petals through his fingers to flutter helplessly after it. Kerchunk! The casket hit the soggy depths of the grave.

"Uh! Uh! Uh!" Lew said. His voice was harsh—guttural—like the cry of a beast.

Mike O'Toole came forward and thrust his shovel into the heap of muddy earth beside the grave. Lew turned and walked away.

Lew went into the city that afternoon and got drunk. No one in Scatterfield had ever seen Lew drunk before. When he got off the streetcar in West Scatterfield that evening, his staggering feet carried him to the post office steps, where he sat down. Old Charlie Heston found him there with his face buried in his hands, mumbling angrily.

Charlie helped him home, and the neighbors came in. They got his big, hulking body into his rickety bed, where he rolled on his back, the straw tick swishing beneath him.

"You better try to sleep," Old Charlie had said to him.

And Lew had fixed him with his fierce, black eyes, dull now with alcohol.

"Religion is the opiate of the masses," he mumbled. And then, bellowing angrily, shaking his fist at the ceiling, "You damned old villain—if you're up there! Ohhhhhhhhh!"

Lew rolled over drunkenly on his belly and buried his face in a dirty pillow. He was soon asleep.

So the old man, moving slowly about his house and garden, unseals minute bits from the vaults of memory. He drags broken parts of an old tale through his head—but without pain. And as Ohio's summer night drops its shroud over Scatterfield, he stands at the corner of the house in his withered, old, bare feet. He shades his sunken eyes with a gnarled and trembling hand, and he scans the sky patiently.

"Rain," he mumbles. "It will rain tomorrow. My sweet corn—my potatoes. We need rain."

He shakes his ancient head as he walks in the back door. It's been a long time—a long time it's been. But bygone things crawl languidly about in the mind sometimes. Anyway, everything seems old and long ago. . . .

Afterword

by Emerson Price

It is a long way back to Scatterfield in the days of old, and the path—of meager proportions—leads blindly through a wilderness of years. The journey is silent and lonely; yet the silence is interrupted now and again by vague and indistinct echoes emerging from the past. The echoes are enfeebled voices of wraiths who no longer have physical substance.

For the characters in this novel—most of them—have long since passed into shadowland. As one might suppose, the characters are composites. Yet in a wider sense they were very real people: certain characteristics of one simply assigned to another. Most of the adventures and misadventures recounted are also real incidents, having happened in one way or another during the author's boyhood and youth. The Scatterfield Gang very largely had its inception in reality.

The town must also be regarded as something of a composite, though the greater base is a wretched place where the author spent boyhood and early adolescence. For various descriptive purposes the author had also in mind a coal mining town—once visited—as it existed sixty years ago.

While the town is now a part of an Ohio city, it remains a slum. Sixty years ago the struggles of the inhabitants with poverty and bleak surroundings were not calculated to stimulate intellectual pursuits. Since most of them have deserted the living, one must wonder what purpose they served in the annals of the human race. That is a question not easily answered. It must remain a riddle, for purposes are sometimes hidden carefully away from human perception.

The way of life in Scatterfield sixty-five years ago—and in the cities as well—has perished from the earth. Only those who grew up with the century retain on the walls of their minds certain images describing the habits of people long ago and the severe restrictions placed upon their lives. All this would be difficult for younger folk to comprehend. Thrust back into it they would face it with the utmost dismay.

Man's best friend was not the dog, but the horse, and literally everyone, whether or not he owned one, was dependent upon these noble animals for making available supplies upon which his life depended. Schools in Ohio's countryside were nearly all one room, one teacher, eight grades. Curiously enough, all who completed the eight grades were able to read and to write, the latter facility, even among slow learners, sufficiently secure that they made themselves understood. The sort of teaching that brought this about seems also lost somewhere as bigness moved in and incompetents—experts, if you please—took over. Many now emerging from modern schools cannot write a simple declarative sentence.

On the completion of eight grades girls cast about for satisfactory husbands; they were described as "good providers." The boys became men instantly and went to work. Among the poor they reproduced themselves at an alarming rate. Few went on to high school, fewer still to college. Yet many highly literate people emerged among them.

Small farms, despite the arduous labor involved, were still profitable; they have since been swallowed up by gigantic business groups. Even a man with a small piece of land could grow a stand of wheat of sufficient size to trade at the mill for enough flour to last him the winter through. Nearly all baking was done at home; baker's bread could be had, to be sure, but it was expensive: four cents a loaf. Day laborers were paid $1 a day, foremen $1.25, and teamsters owning their animals $2. All this and much more clings to the aging mind. Were people happier then than now? One must suspect that life has been difficult in every age, but much more so for some than for others.

The lives of the Scatterfield Gang, as subsequent years affected them, are made clear in this tale—that is, all save one. Mark Cullen, according to plan, was to make an appearance in two subsequent novels. Circumstance denied him this chance, which may be just as well, for he discovered that life is not the puny adversary he had supposed, and so he did not become an enviable figure. Yet many friends who read this novel have asked what happened to him. Well . . . .

He found life in the city very lonely, for he had not the time to make and sustain new friendships. He had had only one ambition, which prodded him only occasionally in earlier boyhood but which became more sharply defined as he grew older. He wished to become a writer, and when bitten by that bug one becomes afflicted by a malady vaguely resembling lunacy. At the same time he was acutely aware that his untutored intellect was by no means equal to the task before him.

Thus, and despite his deep hatred for the confines of school rooms, he entered high school, determined to reduce his intellectual deficiencies. It did not work. Michael Cullen had fallen on evil days with an income so diminished that he could give Mark no financial support. Mark tried to earn needed funds. He was up at 5 A.M. daily to mop out and clean a neighborhood drug store. For this he was paid $2 a week. He became an usher for one of the old B. F. Keith vaudeville houses, afternoon and evenings. Here he earned $4 a week.

A teen-age boy who is abed at midnight each day and up at 5 A.M. is never fully awake, and stumbles about in something of a dream. There was no time for study, and Mark earned a reputation for stupidity among his teachers. This could not go on. He dropped out of school leaving Judy Cullen in tears as she looked at his strapped-up books, never again unstrapped.

Always an avid reader, Mark Cullen now tackled the heavier stuff—Locke, Hume, Kant, Schopenhauer, Freud; he read widely in history, both ancient and modern, and made his way through Gibbon's *Decline and Fall of the Roman Empire*; and he studied some anatomy. He did not neglect fiction, where he learned enough of form to understand that form without substance makes shallow reading. He had a naturally retentive memory, and he read with comprehension. As the years multiplied he acquired his own definition for education: wide reading, experience, and intelligent observation—except in specialized professions such as medicine where the practitioner must continue so absorbed in his own field that he has little time to acquire knowledge in other areas.

As a willing student, he learned a good deal about sex, and he discovered the comforts and delights hidden in the bottle. In his younger years he sometimes imbibed too freely; later his habits became more moderate.

He worked at a great variety of jobs but always made time for reading and for practice in writing. He was for a time a bank clerk; he worked as a rivet heater in a steel railroad-car manufacturing company; he worked in a glass factory before a furnace so hot that one had to wear wool to prevent catching fire. Fifteen minutes before the furnace and a five-minute rest period when one stepped out a door, ducked his head into a barrel of water and sat glassy-eyed for five minutes reviving waning energy. For a time he worked in a labor gang for the Ford Motor Company.

Finally he took a job as editor of a weekly labor paper at a very small salary. But it gave him ample time to do some of his own writing. He was modestly successful, publishing in a number of magazines, including a couple of quality publications. Then came the Great Depression, and the labor paper closed shop.

At this point he became a full-time newspaperman with a metropolitan daily, and soon he was to be regarded by his fellows as an able newsman. His features were always highly praised, and he learned that human-interest stories lie all about us unnoticed. During the years he worked for lengthy periods on two other Ohio newspapers.

A late marriage provided him a daughter who changed his whole life, for he had never before encountered such a wide range of talent in one so young. Her birth occurred during the Second World War. He abandoned his own ambitions, investing in her every hope that she would ultimately accomplish all that had escaped him.

In her teens she became an accomplished musician, having mastered five instruments. And she composed music, providing the words for it. She owned a tape recorder, and she would play her music on guitar or banjo and sing the words. Then she would alter the work for improvement. Her voice had little volume, but the tonal quality was rich and lovely. She painted in oils, worked with watercolors and linoleum blocks. But her final forte was to be writing; and she had acquired a large vocabulary which was always used judiciously. Her mother died during her early teens.

During her second year in college when Mark was approaching sixty he became seriously ill, and she returned home to take care of him. There was now an adult relationship, and they became as close as they had been when she was a child. It seemed to him the happiest period of his life. It was to come to a terrible and terrifying end. Four days before her twenty-first birthday she was killed in an automobile accident. It was a blow from which he never fully recovered. Mark had been doing a weekly newspaper column, doing most of his work at home but required in the office one or two days a week. He never went back to his office desk.

With his life emptied of purpose he is forced to wonder what, if any, purpose there was in his Scatterfield life and his later fruitless efforts. He had become the "Last leaf on the tree in the spring."

As the years continued he suddenly discovered that he was an old man, and as such he came to bitterly resent the yokels who described those advanced in age as "senior citizens" and "golden agers." There is nothing golden about growing old, and the senior citizen—no matter that he might have wisdom and grace of mind—is assigned a very low place on the totem pole in our society. What became of the word "elderly?"

Lest the reader confuse Mark Cullen with the author, let it be known that the author was not an only child, but the youngest of five children, all gone now, save only himself.

With the great changes that have occurred during seventy-four years of life—some of them dire, indeed—small wonder that Mark Cullen feels he has lived in two distinctly separate worlds, neither one related to the other. The Scatterfield he knew so long ago no longer exists, except in memory.

Mark often sits in his big, lonely house, looking over his

wide, deep valley and to the hills far beyond. He is surrounded by silence interrupted only by vague echoes out of the past. Why is it that, moving back into Scatterfield, he remarks a single day very clearly? As a boy he owned a tin box filled with his treasures of a kind that only a boy might describe as treasures. There was a loose tile in the foundation of his home, and this provided a hiding place. He would remove the tile and place the box inside the adjoining tile.

On the day so sharply recalled Mark came home from school, intending either to place something in the box or take something out. He discovered that during the day Michael Cullen had cemented the loose tile securely in place for all time. Mark cannot recall what was in the box, but if the house still stands it has remained hidden away for more than sixty years.

If it ever is found the finder is likely to make some such response as this:

"What the hell is this junk stacked away back here? I thought maybe there was money in it."

Ah, me!

TEXTUAL NOTE

The text of *Inn of That Journey* published
here is a photo-offset reprint of the first
printing (Caldwell, Idaho: The Caxton
Printers, Ltd., 1939). No emendations
have been made in the text.

Library of
American Fiction Series

published titles, as of October 1977
please write for current list of titles

Single Lady. By John Monk Saunders. Afterword by Stephen Longstreet

Queer People. By Carroll and Garrett Graham. Afterword by Budd Schulberg

A Hasty Bunch. By Robert McAlmon. Afterword by Kay Boyle

Susan Lenox: Her Fall and Rise. By David Graham Phillips. Afterword by Elizabeth Janeway

Inn of That Journey. By Emerson Price. Afterword by the Author

The Landsmen. By Peter Martin. Afterword by Wallace Markfield

3 / 9 /

F I c
Pri
Inn